Fearless

Jesse Book 2

Eve Carter

ISBN-13: 978-1490933641

ISBN-10: 1490933646

To my lovely family. You are everything to me.

~*~

CONTENTS
~*~

I am strong, because I've been weak. I'm fearless, because I've been afraid. I'm wise, because I've been foolish.

-Anonymous

PROLOGUE

The Fourth of July 1996

Emily

"What the hell are you doing, Emily?" Frank barked, too loudly as usual. "Who's this asshole? Your secret lover, the one you've been sneaking around with?" He leaned his face, red from drinking, into mine. The stench of hideous bad breath, mixed with alcohol, filled my nostrils.

I pulled back, wrinkled my nose in distaste and took a breath. "Shut up, Frank. You're embarrassing yourself."

I had been casually chatting with a male guest at my best friend Lisa's Fourth of July party. Two hours into the event, my stupid ass of a husband trashed my conversation, drunk, and made a fool out of himself. Again. This was the very reason why we rarely got out and socialized.

The new friend I had been talking with paused, midsentence, and then threw his hands in the air, still clasping his drink. I gave him an apologetic look. He shook his head as he started toward the people milling around the pool bar, women in bathing suits covered with sassy sarongs tied around their hips, men gesticulating with drinks in hand and kids cannon balling into the water.

Lisa and her husband owned a beautiful Tudor style house on expansive grounds, with lavishly landscaped gardens and a pool, in the affluent area of Thunder Ridge, in upstate New York.

The outdoor bar on the pool deck was stocked with every alcoholic beverage imaginable and Frank had already sampled too many. No surprise to me. He'd made a beeline for the bar as soon as we had arrived; smirking when he discovered it was stocked with Heineken instead of his usual, cheap brand. Didn't matter the brand, beer would always wake up the green-eyed monster in him. Every time.

"I'm fucking leaving. I've had enough of this shit. You coming?" he asked.

Sourness stung in the pit of my stomach. "No, Frank. We just got here. We never go out anymore and I'd like to have a fun Fourth of July, for once."

"Suit yourself," he snorted. "I'm fucking out of here. You and your boy toy over there will have a better time with me gone, anyway." He waved his beer can in the air and gave me a watery-eyed glare.

"Just go, Frank. I'm sick and tired of your bullshit, drunken behavior every time we go out. But don't drive. Call a cab."

"I'll drive if I want to."

He swung around to leave and I grabbed hold of his arm. "Frank! Give me the keys."

He wrenched free and shoved me hard. I teetered and reeled back, the solid wall of the house keeping me from completely landing on my back. There were at least sixty potential witnesses at the party. But no one saw.

"Fuck off, bitch!" He tipped his head back to drain the last swallow of beer and stumbled into the house.

Frank behaved like such a jerk every time we were out in public, especially if he imagined, in a fit of jealousy, that I was flirting with other men. And in all honesty, he wasn't exactly a prince at home, either.

I pondered for a second whether to go after him, to force him to hand over the car keys, but knew it would be hopeless and I'd most likely end up on the receiving end of a black eye. Maybe a patrol car would pull him over and arrest his sorry ass. That would teach him a lesson.

I would never call the cops on him, though. We needed him, or rather we needed his income to pay the bills. Things had been tough lately, not only with our marriage, but also financially. Three months ago I was laid off from my job as a secretary and Frank's contractor job...well, let's just say it didn't bring in much. With two kids, and Frank drinking half his paycheck, there wasn't enough left over. We ate a lot of Hamburger Helper, minus the hamburger. If only drinking were a job, then we'd be millionaires.

I bolted into the house, to the family room, where I last saw Jimmy and Jesse, our two boys. I prayed that Frank wasn't serious about driving. I decided to have another shot at getting the car keys before he could hurt himself, or even worse, hurt someone else.

I rounded the corner that led into the kitchen and stopped up short right in Lisa's face. "Hey Lisa, have you seen Frank?" I asked out of breath.

"Yeah, I think he just left with your boys." She blinked, bewildered.

"He took Jimmy and Jesse? Why didn't you stop him?" A hot bolt of fear tore through me like wildfire.

"Well, I'm sorry, Em. I was just about to come and find you… he seemed really upset—"

I flung open the kitchen door and sprinted past several parked cars, down the long curving driveway. Thank God. Frank was still there, fumbling with the key, unable to sink it into the ignition of our old 'beater' car. Jimmy and Jesse were sitting in the backseat and Frank was up front, lolling from side to side in his reckless drunkenness, searching for the ignition. I jerked open the driver's door.

"What the hell are you doing? Are you out of your mind, taking the kids with you when you're stupid drunk like this?" I turned to the kids. "Jimmy, Jesse. Get out of the car. Now!" I yelled.

Jimmy opened the backseat door and pulled Jesse out with him. I shut it and guided the kids behind my back, to safety, using my body as a shield as I backed away from the car.

"You fucking cunt!" Frank screamed and slammed his door shut.

Once I got a couple of yards away from the car, I turned around and hustled the kids inside the house. With my back against Lisa's front door, I sucked in a deep breath of relief and encircled both arms around my two little angels, tears stinging my eyes.

"Jesse, did you brush your teeth yet?" I called up as I ascended the stairs to put the kids to bed.

"Just two more minutes, Mom. Can I stay up a little longer? Pleeease…" Jesse's eyes adored me. I ran my hand over his hair, down the side of his sweet, innocent face, cupping his chin in my hand.

"No, baby. Even though it's the Fourth of July, it's time to go to bed. Go on. Get going." I bent down and gave him a kiss on the top of his head as he buried his pouting face in the soft cotton of my T-shirt. It would be only a matter of minutes before Jesse would be peering at dirt-bike magazines with a little clip-on light he had fashioned himself from various junk items he found on the basement workbench.

Jesse had been infatuated with dirt-bike magazines ever since last summer, when his dad and his uncle, Kenny, took the two boys to the Motocross races and

Jesse had immediately fallen in love with anything that had to do with motorcycles. Of course, Kenny covered the cost of tickets and treats at the race; it had been his idea to take them anyway. That darn Kenny.

I chuckled as I laid my hands on Jesse's shoulders. I turned him around and marched him into the bathroom.

"Teeth, mister." Handing him the toothbrush, I cracked a smile and dug my fingers into his sides.

"Stop, Mom!" Jesse wrenched and squealed. "Don't tickle me…"

I let him loose and caught the reflection of my face in the mirror. Brushing my hair aside, I dabbed a fingertip of extra makeup to hide the purple and red bruises on my forehead and rearranged my bangs to cover them. Jesse finished brushing his teeth just as the doorbell rang.

His little blue eyes lit up. "Maybe it's Daddy?"

I ushered my youngest into bed and trotted down the stairs. Knots formed in the pit of my stomach with each descending step.

I stood up on tiptoes and looked out the small glass window in the door. My peering gaze was met by the somber faces of two police officers, standing on the front porch, wearing dark blue uniforms. I flipped the deadbolt on the heavy wooden front door and opened it a crack.

"Yes…?" My voice was barely a whisper.

"Hello ma'am. Are you Emily Morrison?"

My lower lip quivered and I stepped back, allowing

the door to swing open wider. "That's me. Something wrong, officers?"

"Is your husband Frank Morrison, ma'am?"

"Yes..." I pulled at the fabric of my dark T-shirt with white knuckled hands, twisting it into nervous, angular pleats.

"I'm afraid we have some terrible news. Your husband was involved in an automobile accident this evening. His vehicle ran off the road and hit a tree straight on...he wasn't wearing a seatbelt. His body was thrown through the windshield. I'm afraid he died instantly. We're so sorry, ma'am."

The Fourth of July 1996 was the day the Earth stood still and fell out from under me.

CHAPTER 1

Jesse

"Jesse, are you okay?"

I lifted my gaze. I had been staring, blankly, at the black screen of my cell. I looked into Niki's eyes, still clamping hard on my phone. My pulse increased with every tick of the clock and my breathing came in short puffs.

"I'm okay. At least I think so."

I was anything but okay. I had just learned that the man I thought was my uncle was in fact my father. Everything between the two of us had shifted, in a matter of moments. I was freaking out, but I knew better than to go all ape shit in front of Niki. I had to get it under control. The reality of what I'd just heard on the phone exploded in my mind and shredded my world into a million pieces, bleeding toxic questions that oozed pain into my heart. Who were these people? How could they do this to me? Kenny lied to me, that son of a bitch had fucking lied to me. All this time, right here, straight to my face, just lied. Again and again. And my mom. Fuck!

My mom fucking lied to me too.

Fuck! Fuck! Fuck! I pounded my fist on the cold slab of granite that was the bar's surface. Niki's face reacted and I could see she was alarmed. I didn't want her to see the hurt in my eyes.

I turned away from her, in shame, and closed my eyes, gripping the edge of the bar top at my back. My mind reeled with questions, torqueing like a tornado, trying to restructure every perception I had of my family. My construct of reality was falling apart; pieces that seemed solid and concrete were melting away at an alarming rate. Everything that I thought was genuine and real was churning into a dark, black mush. I wanted to scream. I fucking wanted to rage, break things and throw shit at the walls.

"Jesse, what is it?"

I didn't want to scare Niki with a tirade. She was like an angel to me. She could make a sinner change his ways. Whenever I looked in her eyes, all of my pain eased. It was a mystery to me why Niki had this effect on me when no other girl ever had, but the effect was extraordinary and wonderful every time I got close to her. And right now, I was struggling. I needed her energy to ground me.

I turned back to face her. "Did you hear what the nurse said?"

"Only that you're a match to Kenny, but that's great news…so why do you look like someone just died?

What it is, baby?" She took my hand in hers, leaning across the bar on her elbows.

I wasn't sure if I was supposed to be happy, or angry, or both. And how was I supposed to open the bar in ten minutes when a monumental bombshell had just been dropped on me? It changed everything. My heart began to pound again. I took a deep breath and looked into her eyes for strength.

"You are not going to believe this. It's fucking crazy, Niki. The nurse said that Kenny is not my uncle."

She looked puzzled and cocked her head to one side. "What do you mean? If you're a match, he has to be your uncle."

"He's my fucking dad." The words came out sharply, with a puff of air. I willed my pulse to stop racing. It didn't. Though it was hard news to swallow, no one could argue with damn scientific tests.

Niki's eyes widened and she jolted upright. "Kenny…is your dad?" she stammered. "That's impossible. Are you sure?"

"Straight up. That's what the nurse said. And these DNA tests are a hundred percent accurate. I don't see any way for it not to be true. This is so fucked up."

"Shit, that is…sorry, fucked up. And I thought my family was a mess. What're you going to do?"

"I don't know. If Kenny has known all along that I'm his son… God! This is just one big cluster fuck!" I ran both my hands through my hair and clenched my fists. The agitation was rising again and I needed to get my mind off all of this before I freaked out completely. I picked up some dirty glasses and started filling the dishwasher.

"Let me help you," Niki said. She moved around behind the bar and worked next to me, rinsing glasses, letting a blue silence cool the air.

Niki was like a balm for my aching soul, standing next to me. Her long dark hair swished around her shoulders, each movement releasing a soft delicate scent that wafted to my nostrils. It made me want to touch her and feel her in my arms.

"Thanks, baby. I seriously don't know what I would've done if you weren't here for me." I placed my hands on her hips, looked straight in her beautiful green eyes and softly kissed her forehead. It was working. I closed my eyes and breathed her in, breathed in the serenity she provided me with.

Niki snaked her arms around my neck, holding them out so her wet hands wouldn't drip on my back. "Baby, I'm here for you. Just take deep breaths and calm down. Things will work out."

She pressed her sweet lips to mine and made the world settle back on its axis. My muscles relaxed and the impending rage dwindled.

Turning back to her task, Niki closed the dishwasher and wiped her hands on a bar rag. "You know, Jesse, maybe Kenny never knew about you being his son." She stood with one hand on her hip and the white rag in the other as she talked. "Or if he did know, maybe there was a reason why he kept it quiet. Maybe he was protecting you and protecting your mom's reputation by not telling. Think about it, Jesse. What would that say about your mom…you know… if he told everybody?"

Her words impressed me. I could see why her dad wanted her to be a lawyer. She had an analytical mind for it and the ability to twist things around to fit the opposing argument. She could be right about Kenny; I wanted her to be right, but my emotions still had my head in turmoil and my thoughts tumbling towards disbelief. I was on an emotional roller coaster. One moment my thoughts triggered anger and betrayal, prepared to rip through me, then they would subside as I talked it out with Niki, only to be replaced again by another powerful surge of anger. The shock of it all was still fresh for me and it left me feeling disoriented.

I was silent for a moment. "Maybe you are right. He should be here later today. I just hope he'll finally tell me the truth and not lie to me again."

"Go easy on him, Jess. Remember, he's battling cancer and he's very vulnerable right now. He has a lot to handle." She stroked my upper arm with her petite hand. I looked down into her eyes and felt her compassion.

A clattering commotion jerked both of our heads towards the rear of the bar as Chase burst in, out of breath. "Dude! I know, I know, I'm late, shit…I overslept, big time." He practically fell into the work station behind the bar.

"No kidding, asshole. " I grabbed the white bar rag from Niki and dried my hands. I knew he was stretched thin, working two jobs. I gave him a crooked smile to take the bite out of my words.

"Sorry, man. My bad. It won't happen again." I tossed the towel at him and he continued, "Hey, Niki. What are you doing here? Don't you have a class to go to?"

"Yeah, well, I came to help…"

"And a good thing she did…Somebody had to pick up your slack." I nudged his shoulder in jest. "Hey, cover the place for us, will you? We're going out." I scooped up Niki's purse and handed it to her. She stared at me like she anticipated I would spill the entire story to Chase on the spot. She didn't move and just stood there, holding her purse clutched against her chest.

"Where are we going?" She blinked. I took her purse and slung the strap up over her shoulder.

"What's wrong, Jess?" Chase asked. I took Niki's hand and started for the door. "You seem a little grouchy. Is it your time of the month?" he chuckled trying to make light of my bad mood.

I froze in my tracks and clenched my jaw. Niki pulled up short, still attached to my hand.

"Hey, hey, sorry, man. I was just kidding. Bad time for a joke, I see."

"Tell you about it later, Chase." I turned back to

Chase and when I saw the look on his face I felt like an ass for being so short with him. "I need to get the hell out of here right now. Too much shit's been going down."

I whirled around on my heels and shoved the front door open with Niki in tow, bobbing along to keep up with me as I stormed out the door.

CHAPTER 2

Niki

"Jesse, babe, slow down," I pleaded as Jesse yanked me along the sidewalk. His tense grip on my hand squeezed until it was red. He blew out a breath and clipped his pace to a more normal beat.

"Sorry."

I stole a glance at his face, which was sullen. Jesse shoved his hand through his unruly long locks of hair. Even in his black work polo, with the 'Rookies' logo, he was irresistible. The move uncovered the 'Carpe Diem' tattoo which twitched on his bicep, as if it were as pissed as he was.

We walked on in silence and I peered up into his face every couple of seconds, trying to gauge his anger. It didn't take a detective to figure out he was mad as hell. He'd been royally screwed over and lied to by his uncle. Things just kept going downhill as the day wore on. I didn't like this side of Jesse. His anger made my stomach constrict. My body always reacted that way to tension and anger; if there was a lot of hostility in a room, my body could read it like a Geiger counter.

Jesse stopped in front of the first sidewalk café we came across. "This'll do." He pressed the small of my back and guided me to the outdoor seating area. We slipped into our seats, at a small table for two under a white canvas umbrella, on the sidewalk patio. The waitress delivered two glasses of water. The entire scenario played out in near silence. I picked at some invisible lint on my sundress as I watched Jesse peruse the menu. Is he quiet because he's angry or bored with me?

I couldn't bear it any longer. "I can't believe you are taking this so calmly. I would be freaking out."

"Lately, Niki, I've been fucked around a lot, and when you get fucked in the ass several times...well..."

"Oh-kay, that's a little graphic but I get it. Baby, I admire you for being stoic, covering your hurt, but you need to open up about it. This is what happens every time you face a problem, you get angry, push it down, drink it down, then all those emotions come back later to haunt you. You blow up, punch out whoever, just to be in a fight and let all your anger out on some poor bastard."

Jesse shifted in his chair and laid the menu down. "I know, Niki. I can't stand this shit. It's tearing me apart. Why can't I be like you? You're so level headed. That's why I need you, baby. You keep me on an even keel;

you're my voice of reason."

Jesse strategically took the chair to the side of me, not across the table. He managed to close the little space left between us, so close that he could touch me and get his hands on me under the table. I felt the warm hue of red fill my cheeks as he leaned close and stroked a lock of my hair.

His hand found mine and he pressed his lips against it. I kept my eyes trained on him as he feathered kisses on the back of it. His free hand slipped under the table and traced across my lap, sliding up under my loose sundress, landing on my thigh with a squeeze. "Stop looking at me like I'm naked," I said.

He was silent but his eyes spoke volumes. He raised one eyebrow. My gaze dipped to his tattoo on his arm, his work shirt stretched and strained at the edge of the short sleeve. I tilted my head into his. He gave a soft kiss on my lips, sucking my lower lip in his mouth, pulsing squeezes on my upper thigh under the table.

"Want to be a nasty girl, Niki?" He tugged my lower lip between his teeth. "You know you want to…the way you're looking at me…" He whispered in a low husky voice.

I whimpered a slight moan, lips parted, struggling to maintain some semblance of composure in public. It took every ounce of resistance in me to keep from releasing into him. With laughter dancing in his eyes, he pulled back and left me with my head tipped back, breathless. I straightened up in my chair and cleared my throat.

"Stop it, Jesse. People will see..." I forced my voice to sound even.

He grinned watching me squirm and teased again. "See what? That I can't keep my hands off of you, that I'm crazy about you. What's wrong with that, baby? I want to show you off. Show everyone how I feel about you." I reluctantly pulled my awareness back to the present moment. I cleared my throat and wiped my lips with the back of my hand, peering around the small sidewalk café, cognizant of other people's stares and completely flustered.

I smiled and dipped my head down, entirely aware of his seduction in public. I wrapped my fingers around his and took a sip of water, hoping somehow a glass of Evian would keep the fire inside me at bay until we could be alone. I straightened my dress collar, though my sundress didn't even have one, and licked my lips.

"Focus, Jesse." This guy had me wrapped around his little finger. "Back to the issue at hand...your uncle. What are you going to do about this whole insane mess?"

His expression sobered and his dark eyebrows slanted in a frown. "God, I don't know. Go drink myself blind, then find some unlucky sucker who looks at me the wrong way and beat him down..." He waved a sarcastic hand in the air.

"You're scary when you're pissed," I muttered. At least it was a good sign that he was poking fun at his own behavior.

His mouth twisted wryly. "Just kidding, Niki. Don't worry. I'm trying to find better ways to handle my anger. Remember?"

I wasn't a hundred percent convinced of his new found objectivity, though. I pursed my lips and waited for him to continue.

"I'll talk to him." He leaned his elbows on the table. 'I just hope he's up front with me."

"I hope so too."

A flicker of apprehension coursed through my body and I raked my teeth across my lower lip. "I mean…well, there's something I have to ask. I'm just going to be honest with you Jesse and lay my cards on the table. I don't have the greatest history with men in my life. The most important ones have a way of abandoning me and …suppose you don't get this sorted with Kenny. Then what?"

I looked down, wringing my hands in my lap. It seemed like every time I turned around, men were controlling my life. I didn't have a mother and I didn't have a sister to go to for advice. All I had for female support was Kat, to help give me perspective on things; being the good friend that she was, she was solid. But sometimes, in my life, it just felt like I was unnecessary and insignificant, like I was used then brushed aside, like crumbs on the dinner table after the meal is over. I hoped and prayed that this relationship with Jesse didn't go badly, because I was looking at the dark cloud.

I took a breath and mustered my courage. "Are you going to skip town and leave like everybody else? Head back to New York? I need to know, where do I stand in all of this?"

"Are you fucking crazy? No way. I'm not leaving you, Niki. This is not about me leaving at all. This is about Kenny. He has some things to explain and, depending on what his answers are, it'll determine my future relationship with him. This has nothing to do with us. I have to know if Kenny is a coward or a hero. Like you said, Niki, did he lie to protect me and my mom or did he do it to protect himself? How much does he know? Obviously he knows something, but why lie? I need to figure that out. Whatever it is, the answer makes a world of difference." Disconcerted, he crossed his arms and pointedly looked away. I let the silence hang in the air between us. After a moment, he leaned close and took my hand again.

"Niki, why would you even think that I would leave you? Have I ever said anything that'd make you think that?" He peered at me intently and the sting of anxiety evaporated.

"It's just that I have issues and experience…"

"What experience?"

"Feeling abandoned, emotionally that is. It's an old pattern…feeling rejected, unaccepted, well…unwanted. By my dad. From the time he sent me to boarding school."

"Oh yeah, you told me about your dad."

I was reluctant to add that while away at boarding school, I developed some not so positive 'go to' coping mechanisms myself.

"When people you care about, your own family, don't want you around, it's like you're not even worthy of existing. If I didn't have feelings for you, Jesse, I wouldn't give a damn. But you've got my heart and anybody who gets in there carries a heavy responsibility. If we continue, our bond will grow even stronger. Then I can't afford to have you do something like go back to New York and rip my heart out."

"I'm here for you, baby. I want to be with you every second of every day. Trust me. There'll be no ripping of hearts going on here." He pressed his lips to the back of my hand. I sincerely hoped he was right.

"We should order. Kenny could get back any time and I want to be there when he arrives, see his face and how he reacts."

Jesse waved for the waiter to take our order and moments later we were both picking at our chicken Caesar salads in silence.

CHAPTER 3

Jesse

I was in the process of changing one of the beer kegs at Rookies. It was a pain in the ass. I was wrestling with the connection under the bar when I heard the rattle of the flimsy backdoor. *Finally, Kenny is here.*

Kenny poked his head around the corner into the front bar area. "Hey Jesse, Niki. How's business today? Ready for the happy hour rush?"

I rose and beaded a dead stare straight at him. He appeared so different now, as if the knowledge of him being my father morphed him into a different man.

Kenny's eyes stilled and grew serious. "What's going on? Did something happen here?"

"They didn't call you?" My voice rose slightly in pitch. I closed the door on the cupboard that housed the silver aluminum keg.

"My phone died. Did the hospital call?" He leaned forward anxiously, then pulled back after reading the expression on my face. "Ah, you're not a match..."

"Oh, I'm a match alright," I said.

"Oh God, Jesse, thank you, thank you, that's

wonderful." He took a step forward to hug me but stalled. His elation mellowed. He glanced at Niki then back to me and cleared his throat. "Something's not right. You don't look happy about this news. What is it…what's with the graveyard attitude in here?"

"They said that I'm a match for my dad."

"Your dad? I don't understand?"

"Kenny, they said that the fucking blood test showed that you are my dad. What the hell!" My voice was raised in pitch.

"I…I…don't know what to say."

I was startled at how tired his face appeared. No longer able to look me in the eyes his chin dropped to his chest. His voice strained. "Jesse, I…" He rubbed his face with the heels of his hands and exhaled a long breath. "Oh my dear God, where do I begin…?" He was visibly shaken.

Clenching my teeth together I said, "So…what? Shit just happens? You knew all along, but never found the time to tell me? How fucked up is that?"

I lowered my voice when I noticed a couple of stray customers had roamed in and were waiting for service at the bar.

Niki leaned in to me and lightly laid a hand on my forearm. "I'll go take care of them, you two talk." She ducked away to the other end of the bar where the two men sat. I hadn't heard them come in the door. I was lost in such focused anger a jet could have landed behind me and I wouldn't have noticed.

Kenny threw his hands up and shrugged. "No, I never knew for sure, Jesse. Trust me. Not even your mom did. But honestly? I always had my suspicions."

My heart rate picked up again and I paced the floor in front of Kenny, my hands twitching at my sides as we continued.

"And for some stupid reason you—and mom—decided I didn't need to know? I was not *allowed* to know who my own dad is? Was it so fucking hard to take a paternity test?"

"Calm down, Jesse. Nobody was ever trying to hurt you."

Calm down? I have a damn good reason to be upset.

"I wanted to find out. Years ago, back when I stayed with you after Frank died, but your mom made me promise not to press it further. To keep it a secret."

"Why would she do that to me? Why keep the secret..." An image of my dad flashed into my mind and my throat threatened to hold all my words hostage. "Even after my dad...I mean Frank...died?" Reality hadn't adjusted yet and my mouth couldn't bear to form his name as a reference to 'uncle.'

"I'm sure your mom had her reasons, but that's something you'll have to discuss with her, Jesse. I can't help you there."

My brain was a catastrophic mess. It was all I could do not to say something stupid that I would regret later. Except for Niki, I didn't know who or what I could trust anymore. Life at twenty-four shouldn't be this complicated. My accident ruined my career; Jimmy threw me out and now, to top it all off, the revelation to end all revelations about my dad just screwed up my entire perception of life.

"Tell me the truth here for once, Kenny—Dad. That time after the funeral, after you stayed for more than a year, why did you leave and… what's up with that love letter?"

Kenny raked his hand through his hair and spotted an empty chair in the seating area with tables. Unfortunately, there were a lot of empty seats in Rookies these days.

"Can we at least sit down? I need a drink."

I stomped over to the nearest table and shoved a chair back, the wooden legs screeching as they dragged across the polished cement floor. I sat down hard and crossed my arms across my chest. Niki poured two draughts of Coors light and a JD chaser to go with each. As soon as she brought them to our table, Kenny whisked the shot off the tray, even before she had a chance to set it down. In one swift jerk, he threw it back as if the golden liquid held the fortitude he needed.

Too restless to sit just yet, he leaned over with both palms flat on the table and looked me straight in the eye. "Listen Jesse, nobody else knows about this. Your mom wanted it that way."

My eyes narrowed and I nodded, silently waiting. I'd been lied to long enough; finally, the truth. "Go on…"

Kenny pulled up a dark wooden chair and sat across

the table from me. "Do you remember your grandmother, Donna?"

"Mom's mom? Sure. We used to go visit her every other week until she passed away. I was about fifteen or so. You already told me that she insisted that Mom and Dad... fuck—I mean Frank—had to get married after Mom got pregnant with Jimmy."

Kenny took a long draw on his beer, like it would buy him more time. "Yeah, that's right. So you can imagine, their marriage wasn't exactly a happy one; I mean, with that kind of responsibility being forced on them and all." Kenny pushed the beer aside and worked the fingers of his hands, nervously pulling and twisting them. "A couple of years later, your mom and Frank had a big fight. Frank had been laid off from his job as a construction worker.

"Your mom and dad lived in a small, cheap, second floor apartment with no air-conditioning and Jimmy was just a baby, about a year old maybe. Your mom wasn't working at that time; she stayed home to take care of Jimmy. I think they even had to go on welfare and get food stamps when your dad lost his job.

"I stopped by one night, on my way home from work. I had heard about Frank losing his job and I wanted to check on them. Well...there was Frank, getting ready to go out on the town. Your mom had a basket of laundry on the bed and Jimmy on her hip, when she took me to where Frank was getting ready. He had just showered and was standing in front of the bathroom mirror, putting on cologne, all dressed up in his going out clothes, combing his hair... Man, I couldn't believe it, he was getting all dolled up to go out without her.

"Anyway, she stood there, looking so dejected and hurt, watching him primp in the mirror and that's when I got caught in the middle of their fight. She said to him, 'What do you think you're doing, Frank?' He told her he was going out. She was no fool, she knew he meant going out drinking to the bars, to flirt and probably stay out until morning. It had been happening like that for a while, it's sad to say. So she said, 'You're married, Frank. You're not supposed to be going out partying without me. We have a baby now; you don't get to go out.'"

"What did he say?" I asked.

"He didn't say anything, just kept getting ready. So arrogant...like he deserved it and she didn't, and then he walked out the door. Left her standing there, sweating like crazy in the summer heat of that piss-hole of an apartment, still holding little Jimmy on her hip, tears rolling down her face. She was screaming at him, stuff like how he should act responsible now that he had a kid...and a wife."

"What an asshole." I closed my eyes, hoping the pain that stabbed in my heart would subside. I shook my head. The image of Mom, helpless and crying, rocked me to the core. In that moment, I wanted nothing more than to jump in my truck and drive back to New York to see her. I wanted to tell her how sorry I was, sorry for being a selfish fuck up of a son.

Kenny pulled his beer in front of him, giving his restless hands a place to be still, as he cupped them around the glass. He hung his head and stared at a drop of moisture, rolling leisurely down the face of the beer glass. "Your mom was so used. It destroyed her spirit. She deserved better, should've met another guy—she was so innocent and sweet. Frank took that from her—the bastard." His voice lowered to a hushed whisper. "And he was my fucking brother." He dragged the back of his hand across his cheekbone.

Shit, is he crying? Something in the room sucked all the air out of my lungs and my throat was as tight as a frog's asshole. I averted my eyes and glanced over to Niki, behind the bar, and shifted in my seat. As my nails dug into my jean covered thighs under the table, I blinked hard and cleared my throat.

"Why didn't she just leave him?"

"Didn't have the money, hell she didn't even have a car. She had to take the bus to work, when she did have a job, later. She told me she would take Jimmy to a babysitter first, on the bus, loaded with all his baby bags and stroller, then walk to her work from the sitter's house. She told me later, when the weather was cold—below zero, like it gets in New York winters—she would wait for the bus in a phone booth holding Jimmy, all bundled up in his snowsuit, just to block the subzero wind,."

"I didn't know it was like that. No one ever told me." I said.

""Who would? Who wants their kids to know what a shitty life they had to endure?" Kenny said.

"She never should've married him."

"Your grandmother had something to say about that. She, and everyone else at the time, pressured them to get married, to do the right thing. Shit, what's the right thing anyway? People don't know shit." Kenny spat the words. "Frank was being a total dickhead to your mom. I confronted him about it. He basically told me to fuck off…to stay the hell out of his life, mind my own business."

"Obviously, you didn't." I concluded.

"No, you're right about that one. I adored your mother. Whenever Frank went out to one of his 'parties,' I would get together with Emily. It wasn't until she got pregnant that she panicked. She was scared what Frank would do if he ever found out about us."

"I can see that." I nodded. "Did he ever find out?"

"No, despite our affair, I guess she and Frank… well, you know…she was still *with* Frank, so he had no reason to doubt that the baby wasn't his. I gotta admit I was thrown for a loop. Shit, I was in love with your mom, yet she chose to stay with Frank, despite the abusive behavior. After a while, I couldn't stand to witness all the drama, to watch it eat her up…it consumed her. So I got as far away as I could and moved to California."

I had one more question, one more piece to the puzzle that I needed the answer for. I took a deep breath and dove in.

"So what about that love letter? You said she wrote it much later, after Frank died. Is that true?"

Kenny paused then cringed like a man stung. "Not exactly…"

"Kenny, you promised no more lies…"

"Well…shit." It was his turn to take a breath before he had the nerve to continue.

"After I left, after you were born, she started writing me letters. She wanted me to come back, said she couldn't stand being around Frank anymore. But Jess, it was too late, for me, by then. And besides, there was still the whole issue with your grandmother. She never would've accepted Emily getting a divorce. Remember we were only about twenty-one years old. Your mom needed your grandma's help to take care of you and Jimmy. When I moved to California, I made the decision that, unless your mom and Frank got a divorce, I would stay out of it and stay put here."

Kenny leaned back in his chair like he was exhausted. I stared blankly at the wood grain pattern of the table top. I wasn't aware of how much time had passed while we talked. It was weird. I felt like I'd been sucked into a time warp. I hated to think of Mom being treated so badly, going through so much hardship. I had no idea. No wonder she was depressed. A barrage of emotions overwhelmed me and all I could do was stare and rub a stray water drop from my beer into the faux grain of the table. I needed to process all of this and that would take time.

CHAPTER 4

Niki

"Are you coming to Sara's party, Saturday night?" Kat asked as she formed an 'o' of concentration with her mouth. She drew a brush, loaded with black mascara, along the length of her full lashes.

I looked up from behind my laptop screen and wondered why we women make that shape with our mouths when the makeup's going on our eyes. Kat dropped the mascara wand and traded it for eyeliner. She was good at flicking the end of the line up into a sexy point. I wasn't so good at it. I called my make-up artistry the 'smudged' look. It could be a trend.

"Wish I could, hun, but my dad has demanded my presence at the house Saturday night. It's—Cinnamon's birthday." I had to pause before my mouth would allow her name to come out.

When a person rolls their eyes at a disgusting remark, their speech pattern is interrupted. It's a reflex, because when the brain is disgusted, the mouth cannot properly form words. I'm not making this up. I took a

Linguistics class at UCLA. Okay, that's a bunch of bullshit, but she has a stripper name, for God's sake.

"No way. How old will she be, like 12?" Kat tipped her head away from her eyeliner pencil and spoke to my reflection in the mirror over her dressing table.

From my vantage point on Kat's bed, I could not only see her sitting at the make-up table, but I also saw the vibrantly colored wall on which the mirror hung, a sore reminder that we probably wouldn't be getting our damage deposit back when we moved out.

My dear friend was no stranger to my opinion of my dad's, way too young, second wife. Second wife—geez. It's sad to say, but I had really hoped by now Cinnamon would have smelled the old folks' home on him and I would be referencing his third wife.

"Are you taking Jesse?"

"U-u-m, I haven't exactly told my dad about Jesse, yet." I winced at the thought. "I'm still waiting for the right moment."

Who was I kidding? There'd never be a right moment to introduce Jesse to my dad. They were polar opposites. No way would my dad approve of him.

"Take him. Your dad needs to realize you don't play with dolls anymore. You can make your own decisions about who you want to date."

"I wish. And to make matters worse, I have a feeling Jason will be there."

"Fuck, you're kidding me." She dropped her hand with the eye-liner, spun on her little pink stool and looked straight at me. "Oh, you *have* to take Jesse now, girl. I wish I could be there for that 'cock' fight," she giggled.

"You're a real comedian, Kat," I said dryly. "I get it."

Kat dabbed the corners of her eyes and said, "Who gives a shit what your dad thinks of him, anyway?"

I sighed. She was right. I needed to show Jason and my dad that I've moved on. Besides, I don't think I could face the whole evening at my dad's alone. I needed Jesse's support. Jesse would kill me, though. He would have no clue what he'd be walking into.

I pounded the computer keyboard, entering 'Google' for an internet search and typed: Birthday gift ideas for a 28 year old skanky, bitch-whore stepmother.

Google responded, *"Did you mean – Birthday gift ideas for a 28 year old, Spanks, rich décor, stepmother?*

Hmm. Didn't work.

"Jesse probably won't go anyway, but I'll ask."

Kat ran a quick brush through her long blond hair, jumped up and wrapped her arms around me in a 'best friend' hug. She looked me straight in the eyes. "Niki, promise me, whatever happens, you'll tell me *everything*." She laughed and grabbed her black leather guitar case from beside the bed.

"Listen, hun. I gotta run. I have a rehearsal but I'll see you at four-thirty, right?"

"What's at four thirty?" I asked.

"Jesus, girl. Have you lost your brain this morning?

Simone's, for a mani-pedi, remember?"

"Oh, right." I replied. Kat tucked her chin in and stared at me, one hand on her hip. "I'll be there, already."

"You better show up or I'll spank your ass. I fucking mean it."

"Yeah and I'd probably like it."

She huffed. "Be there or be square." She hoisted her guitar case by the handle and called out loudly, as she left the room, "Where's my purse?" as if expecting the apartment itself to answer her.

"It's in the living room, on the floor at the end of the couch, where you always drop it." There should be an iPhone app for that. Find My Purse, instead of Find My Phone. It would make millions. And with that thought, I heard the click of the front door as it swung shut.

I picked up my iPhone, poked my finger at the letters on the screen, and wrote a short text message to Jesse, inviting him to the party.

Send.

That's it.

The cat was out of the bag.

I glanced at the clock. *Shit*. I was late for class.

CHAPTER 5

Jesse

A shrill ringing pierced my ear drums, alerting me to the fact that, although the blinds were shut, the bedroom was still blazing with brightness. The damn vertical blinds on the window couldn't compete with the intensity of the California sun and I wasn't ready to wake up yet. I groaned. What the hell? The fucking alarm clock was raining audio torture down on me at 9:30 a.m. I jabbed at the pillow, rolling on my side and smashing it over my exposed ear. I wasn't a morning person by any stretch of the imagination. Did I set the alarm last night? I gave up and punched the dismiss button. Silence. Fuck, I'd only slept for a few hours.

I'd been up most of the night, after the bar closed, strategizing how to get my racing career back on track. I had emailed my agent that my hand and leg were healing faster than expected, thanks to Chase's magic workout plan. It was time to start talks with new team managers. If things worked out, I could be back on the circuit within a few months.

I flung the white pillow from my face and it bounced to the floor. Reaching for my cell phone I checked for messages. A shit-eating grin spread across my face. I leaned up on my elbows to read the text from Niki:

"Hey babe, ready to meet my crazy family Saturday evening? There's a birthday party for my dad's wife and I want you to come. Pleeease? I'd rather have a root canal than go to this party alone."

I sprang up to a sitting position, wide awake. Fuck me. Meeting the parents was a big step, maybe too big. Not that I didn't want my relationship with Niki to move forward, but from what I'd learned about Niki's dad, it would be like meeting The Godfather. She had said he was Italian. I hoped he wasn't 'connected.'

Whatever my imagination drummed up, I was pretty sure I wouldn't be welcomed with open arms. Fuck, I'm toast, bloody fucking toast. Who was I kidding? I'd do anything for Niki. The mere thought of her warmed me. Ah shit, I'm such a pussy. But if she needed my support, all the more reason to go. You'll never get much out of life if you don't go out on a limb and risk everything when the right moment arrives. This was one of those moments.

With my good hand I thumbed a reply on my phone: *"I was born ready, baby. Can't wait!"*

Fitness 87 on Fourth St. was practically empty when

I arrived. Chase was already there, finishing up a training session with one of his clients, a sexy, redheaded chick wearing skin-tight workout gear. I particularly appreciated the fact that she wore very little of it. The short top showed plenty of skin and my eyes couldn't help but admire those gym shorts that rode up her butt cheeks just enough for a mouthwatering peek. Each time she shifted her weight, more skin popped out.

I didn't want to interrupt Chase while he worked. I jerked a hello nod in his direction, as he 'spotted' her form while she did reps of arm kickbacks, with a hand held weight. She stood in a wide stance, with her front leg bent and her back one straight, tipped slightly forward at the waist. Chase lightly placed his hands on her torso and instructed her to bend over a little more.

His correction elevated her butt in the air even more, providing an eye-poppingly good view for me.

She parted her lips and blew out a controlled breath as she continued her reps, kicking back her arm with the weight. Turning her head she threw a steamy glance my way and practically undressed me with her eyes. Damn. She was hot and she wanted me. I rubbed my sweaty palms on my gym shorts and darted my gaze around the room, searching for a machine to climb onto. In the past, I would've totally gone for her. Done something crazy, like fuck her brains out in the restroom. But since meeting Niki, I had practically become a saint. Just thinking about fucking this girl made me feel guilty. Or maybe my jaw felt tight because I truly cared for Niki. I needed her touch. She made everything feel so right. But I was afraid, if I told her, she'd run. I hadn't had a good handle on my emotions before I met her. All I'd felt for the last year was non-stop anger. Then I met Niki and things changed. Shit, best to keep my dick in my pants and keep a safe distance. I didn't want to fuck up the best thing that'd ever happened to me.

"Hey, Jesse, I'll be right with you. Last set here," Chase yelled out.

I pawed my hand through my hair and located an available piece of equipment. "No sweat. Take your time, man."

I jumped on a stationary bike for a quick warm-up. I hated getting up early, and late mornings at the gym were the best, not so crowded. Any other time of day, it felt like the entire goddamn population of Los Angeles was a member of *my* gym. Quite the contrast to back home, in Thunder Ridge, where nobody worked out, except for the usual beer lifting exercises, and where the words 'kick-back' meant taking a shot of tequila or some other cheap shit.

The hot redhead's workout ended and she thanked Chase and said goodbye. She pierced me with a smoldering, green-eyed, stare as her peek-a-boo cheeks twitched past me, all the way to the women's locker room. I swore I heard them calling my name, as she disappeared around the corner, but I must have been mistaken. I ignored it.

"How's the hand?" Chase asked as he approached the stationary bike. He wiped his face with a small gym towel. "Good enough to jerk off with?"

"Dude. You're sick. The hand's great, thanks to you, buddy." I took my hand from the grip and high-fived Chase. He retracted his hand with a jerk and examined his palm.

"Gross!"

"You're a bloody magician. I can't believe you managed to heal what three different physical therapists in New York couldn't even make a dent in."

"You did all the work, I was just the guide." He grinned. "It does help when someone is as persistent as you."

"I couldn't have done it without you. Thanks, dude. I owe you big time. What's up with that red-head? I can tell she wants you bad. Let me know if you need help closing." I whistled through my teeth. "She's hot."

"Smoking… And I can handle myself with Savannah, thank you very much."

"Ouww, baby! And a hot name to boot? She's sizzlin."

"Hey, just keep your dick in your pants. You're taken now, remember?"

"Well, somebody's got to be tapping that ass." I laughed.

Chase twirled his little white exercise towel and snapped it at my bicep with a crack. I dodged his aim and the sharp flick missed.

"Peace, bro! I'm just yanking your chain. I'm a changed man, now." I released both hand grips, sat up straight on the bike and stopped pumping the pedals. The whizz of the machine descended in pitch as its revolutions slowed.

"I was up all night, last night. I was so stoked about the progress I've made with my hand and leg. I think I'm ready to ride again, start training." A huge grin spread across my face and I wiped my forearm across my wet brow. "I emailed my agent in New York, told him to start looking for a new team. I can't wait to see what he comes up with." I reached out and squeezed both handlebars at once. "I live to ride, man."

"That's awesome, Jesse. I hope it works out for you. So I guess you'll be out of here before long and back into racing all over the world?"

"It'll be a few more months, but yeah. Have to find a team first and a sponsor to finance everything. It's an expensive sport, Motocross racing."

"So…what about Niki? If you go back to racing, where does that leave the two of you? Remember what I told you; I don't want to be the one picking up the pieces when you decide to go back to New York. Am I gonna have to kick your ass?" He joked and cocked an eyebrow.

"Easy, bro. Niki and I are doing great. We'll work things out. There'll be no pieces for you to pick up. Trust me."

"I hope not. She's one of a kind and I don't want to see her hurt."

"Don't worry. We'll be fine."

At least I hoped so. Niki and I hadn't talked about the future yet and how our careers could mesh. Or not mesh. Damn, I hadn't really anticipated my hand healing this well. I pissed and moaned about my racing career being over, but soon I would have to face the facts. In my pea-sized brain, I envisioned the two of us together; Niki would join me on the road on my racing circuit. But she had art school to attend, her dream to play out. Damn, you know what they say: 'Don't wipe your ass before you...' Shit, oh yeah, and then there's her dad.

"By the way, looks like I'll finally get to meet Niki's family. She's invited me to her stepmom's birthday party on Saturday."

"Fuck, good luck with that. The stepmom's a whack-job biatch." He tossed a pair of leather weight-lifting gloves at me. "Come to think of it, Niki's ex might even be at the party."

"That dude Jason? You mean the overzealous, pompous, vexatious asshole that Niki dated before me?" I had thought he was out of the picture a long time ago.

"My, my, what big words you have. Niki's intelligence must be rubbing off on you. Why don't you just say, 'douchebag?'"

"Okay. Why would that *douchebag* be there? Her

dad knows they broke up."

"Trust me, Niki's dad will use any means necessary to get those two back together. He's a control freak about Niki's life and his number one choice is Jason. Sorry, bro."

"That old timer really needs to take himself the fuck down a notch."

"Just be careful with him. He is a lawyer. And lawyers have no scruples."

"Let him bring it on." The words shot out of my mouth from instinct. "I'll go head to head with Jason *and* Niki's mother fucking lawyer dad. I'm ready to take down the fort for her. I'll show them that!"

"Easy, tiger." Chase held up a gloved hand, palm out. "Just don't whiz on the electric fence." He wiggled his fingers into the other black weight-lifting glove.

My eyebrows furrowed. "What the hell does that mean?"

He chuckled. "Just don't do anything stupid, man."

I kicked a heavy gray dumbbell, resting on the floor. Niki was my everything and it didn't take much for me to spring to her defense.

"And good luck with that birthday party." He squatted to the floor in front of a barbell and easily 'clean jerked' a weight heavy enough to pop my groin muscle from here into next week. "Enough talk, bro. Let's get started."

We continued our training session for an hour and a half, repeating sets on various kinds of workout equipment, focused on building strength in my legs. As we headed to the locker room, Chase turned to me. "How is it going with Kenny, by the way? Did he start chemotherapy yet?"

"Yep, two days ago. He's hanging in there, but man, chemo is brutal. The stuff they gave him, it's pure poison to the human body."

"I know. That's some serious shit but serious shit is what it takes to kill those cancer cells before they kill him."

I nodded and pulled my workout shirt off over my head as I sat on the bench in front of the open locker. I finished changing out of my workout gear and stuffed the sweaty clothes into my gym bag. "Hope he can handle it. I doubt we'll see him at work much. I told him we'd cover most of his shifts and not to worry. "

"Of course, no problem, we'll handle the bar." The metal of the locker door rattled as Chase slammed it shut. "Damn…good thing you decided to come to California. Otherwise Kenny would've been six feet under."

The musky stench of the men's locker room faded away as we wove our way around wooden benches toward the exit doors. I held open the glass door at the front of the gym and allowed Chase to pass ahead of me. "Yeah, life has a strange way of turning out, sometimes. It would suck to have my dad die right after finding out that I actually have a dad who's alive." I snorted. How ironic. "That's why I always say…" I lifted my bicep with the tattoo. "…Carpe Diem."

We were at Chase's car, in the parking lot, by now, gym bags slung over our shoulders. Chase wasn't laughing at my lame joke, not even a smirk. He paused at the driver's door and aimed his key fob at the handle.

"Listen, I wanna talk to you about the bar." His jaw tightened and I stepped around to his side of the car, anticipating a heavy conversation before we got in. "It's no secret we need more customers to make it profitable again. And it doesn't help that Kenny isn't going to be around much. Maybe we need to advertise, pay for some ads in those coupon books people get in the mail."

Chase was right. Lately, even the regular patrons had diminished. The worry on his face deepened as he rubbed at a dent in the door of his old Camry. My eyes followed the movement of his fingers as he poked at a crevice in the paint. I had never really noticed how ghetto his car looked until now. He worked two jobs, yet didn't have enough for a better ride than this. His concerns about the bar were well founded. Shit, who wants to hang out in a bar with a graveyard atmosphere? We needed a marketing plan, pronto, that would put some life back in Rookies and make it the favorite neighborhood hot spot.

"That's a bitch alright, but there's no money for ads. Every cent Kenny has saved will be eaten up by this cancer treatment."

"Damn, I figured as much. I hope I'm not going to

be out of a job in a month. I need this income, you know."

"You and me both." My fears for the bar were the same as his, but I kept a poker face; I didn't want him to get skittish and bail on us. I sure as hell wouldn't blame him if he did but, on the other hand, I didn't want to let him down either. He had been an employee at Rookies since it opened and had loyally stuck by Kenny and the place. *Fuck*. One more responsibility to heap on my shoulders right now. "Things will work out, bro."

He flipped up the door handle on the back door and tossed his gym bag into the back seat and held it open for me to do the same. I tagged his upper arm with an affectionate slap and said, "Worst case scenario, I'll hire you as my personal fitness trainer when I'm back on the racing circuit."

CHAPTER 6

Niki

"Are you sure I look okay?" Jesse stretched both arms out at his sides as he stood in the living room of my apartment. I was getting ready for Cinnamon's birthday party and Jesse had just arrived to pick me up.

"You look great, baby. Don't worry about it." It was so cute. This was the first time I had seen Mr. Self-confident appear nervous. He looked panty-dropping hot in his black jeans and black T-shirt, that stretched tight across his toned chest muscles. Printed graphics in gray swirled across one shoulder and onto the front of the shirt, with a hint of a metallic shine reflecting off the design as he moved. And then there were those dangerous locks of hair falling in his eyes. He reeked of 'bad boy' and I wrinkled my nose, with a mental 'bwah-ha-ha.' He looked so damn hot in that shirt, like a rock star. His bad to the bone looks were sure to raise an eyebrow or two from the Brentwood crowd at my dad's house, who would all be wearing polo shirts with golf motifs. Boring.

I couldn't tear my eyes away from his hotness. There

was not a rational thought in my head and I nearly blurted out, 'Come on Jesse, bend me over, pull my hair, whisper dirty things in my ear and…' But we were late and ripping the clothes off that gorgeous body would have to wait until later.

I groaned and spun on my heels to rush back to finish my makeup in the bedroom. As I sat at the dressing table, my eye caught some movement in the mirror. Then the heat of a body behind me announced Jesse's presence before I looked up. The lip gloss wand tumbled to the makeup table. I felt his hand on my waist. I turned my head to the side, casting my eyes downward. The warmth of his palm slid up to my shoulder and his other hand swept my long hair to the side. A shiver tickled my skin as he slowly lowered his lips to my neck. Lightly, his mouth brushed against me as his hands circled my body, locking me in an embrace.

"We should hurry, babe." He mouthed the words against my neck. "Don't want to be late the first time I meet your dad. They'll think we're not coming."

I closed my eyes and a pleasurable moan lulled in my throat. "You are making this really hard." I exhaled. Still locked in a bear hug, he gently rocked us side to side.

"Hard?" I could feel his mouth smile against my neck. "Hold that thought for later." He pulled his head up out of the crook of my neck, where he had been nuzzling me, and crossed the room. "We'd better get going."

"It'll be fine. Trust me; we are not missing anything exciting by being a little late."

I shut off the bedroom light, checked my makeup again in the hallway mirror as I passed it, and grabbed the birthday gift. Soon I was sitting next to Jesse, in his huge black pickup truck, on our way to the birthday party.

Brentwood was the next town over from Santa Monica but, in this part of California, all the cities had merged together over the years due to massive urban sprawl. If it weren't for the welcome signs, posted at the city limits, a person couldn't tell when they left one area, to enter the other. In the older neighborhoods, the lanes of the streets were uncomfortably narrow. Streets that were intended to accommodate only one car width had been expanded to two lanes over the years, as the population grew. It was almost comical driving Jesse's lifted pickup truck in an area dominated by German engineering; low slung Audis nestled next to the curb, parked alongside sleek BMWs and flashy Mercedes.

After driving up a steep hill, on the private road which led to the stately house, we rolled up in front of the ornate black wrought iron gate of my childhood home, the one I had just moved out of at the beginning of summer to move into an apartment with Kat. It was a modern traditional estate, situated behind gates, on a large lot in the Mandeville Canyon area of Brentwood. Nestled among other four to five thousand square foot homes, it boasted an ultimate 'great room' with vaulted Birch ceilings. When I was a child, I loved how the wood made me feel like a little bit of the trees from outside were inside where I played. The grounds around the house were equally amazing: a wonderful pool house, a six-stall barn, a tennis court, for the time in my life when I thought I wanted to be a tennis pro, a guest house with an office, where Dad sometimes worked from home, and a life-size chess board, built right into the grass with black and white squares of cement.

With his mouth hanging open, Jesse gawked at the sight of the place. "I had no idea...I'm impressed." He pushed the down button on the truck door and the rumble of the engine filled the air as the window smoothly retracted. He stared blankly at the intercom speaker box for a moment, like he was about to place an order at the drive through. He looked a little pale.

"You okay?"

Eying the keypad on the box he asked, "Do I just press the button?"

"No, wait. I have the code to open the gate," I chuckled.

The lift kit on Jesse's truck made it too high to reach the keypad from inside, so I jumped out and ran around the front of the car. I entered the four digit code and climbed back in the truck, as the gate rattled and opened slowly.

I pursed my lips and sucked a breath in through my nose. "It's show time." Although my focus was straight ahead, I saw Jesse nod in my peripheral vision.

As we drove up to the house, the driveway was packed with several other cars. Must be some of Dad's lawyer friends. I could tell by the makes and models which belonged to lawyers and which belonged to Cinnamon's ditzy girlfriends. Pretty sure the brand new Porsche belonged to one of Dad's clients. Then my vision settled on a familiar outline. *Fuck!* Jason's car was there too. I looked at Jesse.

"Looks like my dad invited Jason; that's his car."

"This should be amusing," he said dryly.

"Yeah, define amusing." I gripped the handle of the pink gift bag with white knuckles as Jesse pulled the truck to the side of the long driveway, behind the last car in line.

"God, I can't believe he did that. What a manipulative…"

This was going to be really awkward for Jesse. Pangs of guilt shot through me as I realized the situation I had put him in.

"Don't worry. I can handle Jason. It's your dad I'm worried about." A smile tugged at the corner of his mouth. "He doesn't own a shotgun, does he?"

I let out a breath "Okay, now you're freaking me out." I laughed. "No guns, it's his wife that I'm most worried about."

He slammed the truck into 'park' and reached for the door handle, then paused. "Hey, wait. How will I know which one is Cinnamon?"

"Her boobs will greet you before she does."

"Oh crap." He shoved his hand through his hair. "Let's do this." He kicked open the door then popped up on my side of the truck and gallantly opened my door to help me out.

We were within ten feet of the porch when the front door sprung open and out came Cinnamon with a high cheek boned, slender, trendy looking guy with black lined eyes, Adam Lambert style. They laughed loudly, like something she said was the wittiest remark ever. Her brain was incapable of housing witty remarks. It looked like she and 'Adam Lambert' were sneaking out for a cigarette.

Dad didn't know she still smoked. A few years ago he bought her a new, flashy, convertible BMW, when she had promised to quit smoking. *That* didn't last long. Before the ink was dry on the sales contract, she developed the habit of sneaking out, whenever she could, for a quick smoke. She had the backbone of a snake.

"Niki, baby!" She squeaked in surprise, her long blonde curls bouncing as she started. So glad you could make it." She pulled the front door shut behind her. Her spiky silver high heels clicked on the stone pavers as she baby-stepped her way back to her friend's side. The short, tight fitting, red dress she wore was so tight it hobbled her, and forced her to take little short steps when she walked. The dress had various geometric 'cutouts' that showed off the dark tan of her skin and covered only the most essential areas.

"Cinnamon, I'm hardly your baby." I rolled my eyes. "Please refrain from using any such terms of endearment, for my sake."

She waved her hand in the air in a dismissive manner and tipped her head sideways toward her friend. "She's always in a grouchy mood."

Jesse's eyes were wide as saucers and glued on a pair of boobs that nearly had as much square footage as the house. No doubt he was thinking how huge they were. I didn't blame him. Everyone had the same reaction. They *were* huge, actually, huge as planets. Complete with their own gravitational pull.

"Who's your friend, Niki? Is he my birthday present?" Jesse had managed to unglue his eyes and was kicking an imaginary rock. She looked him over with flirtatious eyes, threw her head back and laughed like a horse. God, I hated that laugh.

"Cinnamon, meet Jesse; and no, he is not your present. He's with me." I shot her a cold glare and hung both my arms around Jesse's neck.

"Jesus, girl. No need to be all territorial. I was just joking," she teased as her gaze raked him up and down.

Jesse turned on his charm. "So nice to meet you, Mrs. Milani. I've heard great things about you. May I wish you a very happy birthday?" He extended his hand.

Oh, he was good. Way to go, Jesse. I'd never heard him smooth talk like that before.

"Oooh, the pleasure is all mine, darling."

It was not only my stepmom who stole lusty glances at Jesse. Her Latino friend certainly claimed his share as well. "Cinnamon, who's your friend? You haven't introduced us yet. Is he your choreographer from Vegas?" She turned slightly towards him. "Oh, sorry. Carlos, this is well…my step-daughter, Niki. Carlos is a friend of mine from Vegas. He came for my birthday and…" She dipped her fingers into the cigarette purse and pulled out a tightly rolled joint between her forefinger and thumb. She hunched up her shoulders like she had a secret. "Carlos and I were just coming out here to…have a little fun." She wrinkled up her nose and smiled. "Want to join us?"

"Oh Jesus. No, Cinnamon. But hey, knock yourself out there, birthday girl." I gave a nod to Carlos and pulled on Jesse's arm. As usual, Cinnamon had made a memorable first impression.

We pushed past the two of them before Cinnamon could get her claws, or her overly pumped up lips, on Jesse. That woman had had more work done in her young life than a 1950 Buick. As we entered the house, I heard her say, "Carlos, hun. I totally forgot my drink in the house. Do you mind getting it for me while I light this shit up?"

We hadn't gotten much farther than the hallway before I heard a voice behind me. "Niki. It's about time you showed up. I was afraid you wouldn't make it. You know I don't like it when people are late."

"Dad!" I started and turned around. I guess I was a little on edge, but he had that effect on me. We gave each other a stiff hug. He was impeccably dressed in a fine suit. Yep, he sure had a client or two here tonight. "Sorry we're late, Dad, but we had to pick up Cinnamon's gift on the way." I lied.

"Oh, I see. No problem then." He looked at Jesse as if he hadn't noticed his presence until now. He squared his shoulders and said, "Who is your friend? Doesn't he talk? Is he mute?" Before I could answer the rude questions, Jesse cleared his throat.

"Mr. Milani, not at all, sir. It's a true pleasure to meet you. Niki has told me so much about you. I'm Jesse Morrison." He extended his hand like a gentleman, but my dad ignored it.

"Jesse Morrison." He narrowed his eyes, as if mentally scanning a list of fugitives' names from America's Most Wanted. "Hmm…Tell me, Jesse. I've never seen you with Niki before. Are you from around here? Your accent sounds a little East Coast."

"Great observation, sir. Born and raised in New York. I've only been here a short while."

"So how did you get to know Niki?"

Geez, it was like the Spanish Inquisition. I figured I'd better run some interference and interrupted, "Chase and Jesse are friends, Dad. Enough with the questions, already. He's not on trial here." I furrowed my brow. I'd had a feeling things were going to go like this. "I brought Jesse as my date, so can we please move on?"

"Really? Well, that is really kind of…"

I didn't want to argue any longer. It was futile. There was no winning or making him understand. I grabbed Jesse, leaving my dad mid-sentence, and continued into the main living room to get a drink. God, I sure needed one.

"That went great." Jesse joked.

"Trust me, that was nothing. Just a typical day around here." I was fuming.

The great room was large, with a massive black Steinway piano as a center piece. For the birthday occasion there was a bar set up against the wall, with wine and beer, and some finger food. I made a beeline directly for the bottle of Chardonnay, strode over and poured a glass to the brim. Before I was able to take a sip, I cringed with the recognition of the voice behind me.

"Hello, Niki."

I turned and saw Jason, standing there, chewing on a crescent roll.

To fortify my nerves, I took a large gulp of my wine. "Hi, Jason. What are you doing here?"

"Your dad invited me. It would have been rude of me to not comply."

I opened my mouth, about to explode into a verbal tirade against Jason. With one hand on my hip and the other pointing my Chardonnay in Jason's face, Jesse came to the rescue and jumped in to diffuse the conversation.

"Hey, Jason, I've heard so much about you. Nice to put a face to all that information."

"So, who are you?" Jason asked.

"I'm Jesse, from New York." They shook hands and Jesse slung an arm across Jason's shoulder, maneuvering him towards the patio as he continued. "So you work for Mr. Milani? That must be cool. I always wanted to know what it's like to be a lawyer. Do you ever…" Their voices faded as Jesse hustled him out to the patio.

Left alone, I breathed a sigh of relief. That was a smooth move on Jesse's part. His diversion gave me a little time to strategize what to do next.

Less than a minute later Jason stormed in from the patio in a huff, red in his face, scowling.

"Niki, I have to leave. Please tell your father I'll see him on Monday, at the office."

"Sure…bye." I mumbled as my eyes followed him out the front door. My head snapped back to the French patio doors, were I saw Jesse entering the room grinning from ear to ear. "What did you say to him? He was all flustered."

He shoved a hand through his hair, pushing back the stands that fell in his eyes. He brushed a gentle kiss across my forehead and put his arm around my waist. "Um… I just told him a story about this guy I once knew who suffered a broken nose after stalking his ex-girlfriend."

I rotated my body to face him, remembering how

those unruly locks of hair drove me crazy, wanting the velvet warmth of his kiss. He locked both arms around me and I poked a finger at his chest as I said, "Wow, you are one crazy boyfriend, Jess." I looked up into his dazzling blue eyes. "But I gotta say… I like it."

"Happy to be of assistance," he chuckled.

Parting my lips, I raised on my toes to meet his kiss.

Before our lips could meet, my dad stormed into the great room, waving his arms in frustration. "Niki, Jason just left in a hurry. Said something about your friend here threatening him. What was that about?" He snapped his gaze toward Jesse. "Threats like that could land you in jail, son."

"Dad, calm down. Jesse just told Jason it would probably be best if he left since I felt awkward with him here."

"Akward! I'll tell you what's awkward, Miss Milani. Awkward is you bringing a date to *my* party when you know your boyfriend, Jason, will be here." He cocked his head and raised an eyebrow, as if we were having some kind of a jousting competition and he just landed a good one.

"Dad… *Father*…Jason and I broke up weeks ago. I already told you that," I said flatly.

"Broke up? Why it sounded more like an insignificant lover's quarrel, than a break up, to me. Surely you are mistaken, Niki. As usual, you don't know what you're doing…"

"And I'm sure *you*, in your infinite wisdom, will tell

me how to run my life."

"Quite frankly, Niki, I do know what's best for you. You're young and foolish and make rash decisions all the time. First you go chasing after some silly fashion design dream and now this kind of immature behavior."

My mouth gaped with indignant surprise. "I thought you were behind me on my fashion design classes. I thought you said taking a year off college would be a good thing…"

Oh my God, poor Jesse. I brought him here, to this dysfunctional family birthday party, and now he was caught in the middle of an argument between me and my dad. He fidgeted nervously, looking as if he wanted to jump in the fight and defend me, but I figured nothing good would come of that.

I threw him a glance and then swept my eyes to the door, hoping it would keep his fighting instinct at bay and we could get the hell out of here.

"That was just a bunch of mumbo jumbo to appease you until you came to your senses and went back to pursuing a real education."

"Really? Did you really just say that? Okay, that's it!" I threw my hands up in the air. "We are leaving, Dad. I can't believe you're doing this right now."

I took Jesse's hand and started towards the living room and the front door.

"That's your answer to everything, Niki, isn't it?" My dad's voice rose in pitch as he followed after me. "I understand now, why Jason broke up with you. As always, if things don't go your way, you run away and hide. Just like your mom did."

I froze in my tracks, like a bird dog on point, and turned to face his horrible accusations. The sharp edge of his words stung my heart, threatening to corrode the precious and delicate memories I had of her, like acid poured on her photograph.

I lunged at him, hitting him flat on his chest with my open hands as hard as I could. "Don't you fucking dare talk about Mom like that! If she hid, it was to get away from you, you brute!"

Tears stung at my eyes, but I didn't want to turn into a sobbing idiot. I wanted to show him that I was strong and confident, that I wasn't going to live my life intimidated by him, crumbling into an emotional mess at his command. My voice cracked a little, but I pulled myself together. "Mom was a saint. Don't you dare tarnish my memories of her with that kind of talk." Dad had an insidious way of implying things, saying just enough to get in my head and make me doubt myself, as if somehow my mom really was to blame.

"Niki, you don't know everything that happened. I tried as hard as I could to help her, but she wouldn't let me."

"Yeah right." I gave a sarcastic short laugh. "What I remember is that you were working all the time, spent hours at the office just to be away from us. The rare moments you were here you avoided her like the plague. Like it was her fault she got sick. You were never there for her, or me, and thanks to you, I still have to go to therapy."

"Niki, I'm aware of that. I pay the bill—like I pay all your bills: your college, your rent, your car, everything! I do it because I know what's best for you. And you think you know everything, but you don't know what drives me. You don't think it was hard for me when your mother died? You don't think I hurt too?" His eyes flashed and his face contorted in anguish as the words spilled out.

"Nice to know, Dad. Your only child was just a big inconvenience for you."

"Niki, I…"

"You couldn't handle my reaction so you sent me away, just swept the problem under the rug, got rid of it—out of sight, out of mind."

"Yes, yes! I couldn't handle your hurt and mine. When you started that cutting phase of yours, I resigned. I gave up. I do sometimes blame myself for the way I handled that. But look at you now, Niki. Your choices will be your undoing and it's your own fault. You decided to move out this time, I didn't send you away. You made the decision to move into an apartment with that singer wanna-be friend of yours."

Oh, now he was pulling out all the stops. First he attacked my choice of boyfriends and now he was insinuating that my friends were losers. I can't make a good career choice, boyfriend choice or friend choice. What's left? I may as well not even exist.

"Now, let me tell you something, Daddy dearest. I chose to leave because I refused to be under the same roof as an egocentric ass who thinks he can control me like some stupid employee...the way you control your precious golden boy, Jason. You know what? I used to think the two of you were so much alike. Now I know better. Jason is an angel compared to the monster you've become. No, I take that back –the monster you have always been!"

For once, my dad was speechless. For a split second, I had managed to shut the lawyer up and, from the look on his face, I think I unsettled him. Before he had a chance to regain his focus, I stormed out of the house, as fast as possible, with Jesse on my heels. I sprinted down the driveway to the truck and within seconds Jesse's big wheels screeched out through the gaping jaws of the black wrought iron gate.

CHAPTER 7

Jesse

What the fuck just happened back there? Niki looked totally pissed off; she was fucking fuming. She sat next to me in the front of the pickup as I drove us back to her place, with her arms folded across her chest and her eyes shooting daggers at…well, I imagined at images of her dad in her mind.

His face was classic when she gave him a wallop on his chest like that and stood her ground. Way to go, Niki. I had never seen her like that before, confident and feisty. I liked it. It kind of turned me on. I mean, her dad was acting like a total dickhead; he sure knew how to push her buttons.

The drive back to Niki's place was completely silent. I shot a glance over at her, every once in a while, to check on her. I didn't want anyone breaking my baby's heart, not even her dad. *Ah shit*. Her eyes were wet. I couldn't stand to see Niki cry. It caused a funny twisting feeling in my stomach.

I took one hand from the steering wheel and reached

over to nudge her arm. The way she had them folded so tight it would have taken a crow bar to pry them loose. "Hey," I said softly and nudged again. She tilted her head my way and released her death grip, letting her arm fall to the seat. I laced our fingers together and squeezed lightly. She wiped the back of her other hand across her cheek.

"You okay, baby?"

She nodded. With her head still titled in my direction, a little smile crept across her face.

I nosed into a space in the parking lot of her apartment and killed the engine. Neither one of us moved. We just sat for a minute. Niki stared straight ahead and then closed her eyes. She popped them open and turned her head toward me and said, "Jesse, I think I need to see a therapist, like right now!" I froze up inside. Damn, this was worse than I thought.

I looked straight at her, "You wanna go to your therapist *now*?"

"I need to see *your* therapist—Jack...Jack Daniels. You may have heard of him? Let's go to Rookies. I need a freaking drink."

I exhaled and laughed. "Shit, Niki, you scared me. I thought you were serious there for a minute..." That was the best goddamn fucking idea I'd heard all night. I cranked the engine, threw it in gear and headed for Rookies.

The parking lot in front was nearly empty and, as we entered the bar, it was unusually quiet. Except for a young couple, making out in one of the booths, we were the only people there. Damn, not a good sign for the health of Rookies.

Chase came out from the back and greeted us with a smile when he recognized us. "Fuck. It's just you guys. I was hoping it might be a customer."

"Nice to see you, too." I flipped Chase the middle finger, out of Niki's line of sight.

"Jackass," he mumbled with a playful smirk.

"Works for me, dude, we *are* customers." I pulled a stool close, smoothing the palm of my hand over the black vinyl seat where Niki's perky little ass would sit. Self-restraint was never my strong suit. "Niki, slide up on this stool here, babe." I ran a hand down over her ass as she stepped up beside me. "And line up some shots, will you, Chase?"

I sneaked a glance at her ass as she perched herself on the stool. Chase laughed and slammed three shot glasses on the bar top. "So, how was the birthday party?"

Niki and I looked at each other, then answered at the same time.

"Don't even ask..." Niki held up a hand.

"Uh, er, well...shit." We both broke out laughing. I let her answer.

"Let's just say...it *sucked*. And leave it at that." Niki pulled a shot glass toward her and ran a finger around the edge, waiting for us to all drink at the same time.

"It went oh-kay," I stressed the second syllable of

the word and gave Chase a look that really said, 'no, it was a disaster.' "Except maybe for the end, where we were chased out of the house."

Chase gave me a knowing nod and, being the clever guy that he was, decided not to inquire any further. I knew Niki was still hurting on the inside. *God*! If he weren't a lawyer and would probably sue me, I'd have taught him a lesson or two for causing her so much grief. Best to let it rest. I changed the subject.

"Still no customers, huh?" I asked.

"Nah, it's like a graveyard here tonight. Five people total. Not good for any night, but a disaster for a Saturday."

"Damn. We need to do something soon or Kenny's bar will be gone by the time he finishes the chemo. I feel like we should print some Happy Hour fliers and hand them out at the promenade." I raked my hand through my hair.

"Good luck with that. That might bring a customer or two, but the only thing guaranteed to work is a big newspaper ad, but that'd cost at least a couple grand."

I drummed my fingers on the bar top. "Newspaper…you just gave me an idea." I scooped up one of the glasses of Jack. "I'll tell you later. Let's kill this shot." We each lifted a glass in a salute.

"Here's to bending over and taking it, Hollywood style." Then all three of us downed it. Niki sputtered and coughed. She stuck her tongue out, making a 'yuck' face.

"A-a-h, that's awful!" She coughed out the words. She still needed some practice at taking shots, but that was okay. I preferred that she didn't drink like a sailor. I threw down a twenty and Chase lined up another round of shots. I wanted to use this chance to talk with Niki alone, so I grabbed our two glasses while Chase went in the back. We sat down in one of the booths in order to have a little privacy.

"Here's to new beginnings," I said, raising a glass.

"New beginnings!" Niki replied and took a glass and emptied it down her throat. It was so goddamn cute the way she twitched her face in distaste at the liquor.

She plopped the glass down on the table and held up a hand. "Okay, okay, enough for now. You don't want me puking all over your truck seats later."

I shoved our empty shot glasses aside and snaked my hand between our beer chasers to reach for hers.

"If the toast we just made was to new beginnings with my family, I assume you were being sarcastic. What a disaster. I apologize for Cinnamon's ogling. I was about to stab her with my high heel. And my dad…I can't believe my dad acted so stupid."

"What did you expect?" I asked.

"I don't know. Anything but that…but I should have known better. He's never liked any of my boyfriends, except Jason of course."

"How long were you guys together?"

"Only a few months and I wouldn't even call it being together. It was all Dad's idea."

"Yeah, I got that part."

I didn't want to talk about that fucker, Jason. Something else her dad had said had caught my attention and had been burning a hole in my mind. I fumbled around, trying to think of a way to bring up the subject. "Your dad mentioned something...I wasn't sure if I heard it right...he used the words 'cutting phase.' Baby, is that the kind of cutting I think it is?" I lowered my voice and looked into her face, trying to read her expression. I gently rubbed my thumb over the back of her hand as I held it.

Niki didn't answer right away. Her face was clouded with despair. She looked down into her beer as if the answer were buried in it.

"It was something that happened a long time ago. I don't really want to talk about it tonight."

I squeezed her hand and looked into her beautiful green eyes. "You know you can tell me everything, right?"

She squeezed back in response. "I know, and I'll tell you everything one day. I promise. It's just that it's something I have been working a long time to forget. Get out of my mind. And then, one stupid evening with my dad and everything comes crashing back."

Tears were rolling down her cheeks. I felt sick to see her hurt like that. I got up from my seat, slid in her side of the booth next to her, and held her in my arms.

"Baby, don't cry. We'll fix this. Whatever it is, I'll help you get through it. I promise. You'll never have to face anything alone again, ever."

She held her gaze on mine. I cupped her face and wiped away the tears with my thumbs. She was so beautiful. Holding her delicate face in the palms of my hands, I felt so unworthy of her grace. I had no idea why she would want a sorry ass dirt bike rider like me, but I wanted to make this woman happy more than anything in the world. She had come into my life and changed me for the better, helped me with my demons, and now I wanted to help her with hers.

She closed her eyes and parted her lips, inviting. I kissed her lips and felt a surge of desire rise within me. But this time, for the first time, I also felt like we were one, like her heart had opened and she was letting me in. It was the most awesome rush of energy. I had never felt it before; it was like the wind gushed in behind me and pushed my soul into hers, melding the two of us together. And it was magical in there with her, calm, serene, beautiful and sweet. Kind of like one of those dreams, in which Earthly words aren't vivid enough to describe the experience.

She whispered into my ear, "You can take me home now, but I want you to hold me like this all night."

"Sure, baby."

We ditched Chase and five minutes later we were once again driving toward Niki's place. I had flipped up the center console, and converted the seat into a bench, so Niki could sit next to me. Her head rested on my shoulder as we drove. It was late and the streets were quiet. I loved it when she wanted to sit close to me. There were times when I fucking craved her company. When? Pretty much any time of the goddamn day. Her sweet face lit me up every time I saw her. And I found it hard to keep from touching her and stroking her face, or arms or… yeah, ass. I couldn't help it. I was a horn dog guy. We men are wired like that. Well, that was my professional opinion anyway. I couldn't stop mixing up sexual thoughts with thoughts of fondness, when it came to Niki. I tipped my head down and gave her a little kiss her on top of her head.

At the apartment we climbed the stairs, hand in hand. Then, without making too much noise, we tiptoed into her bedroom hoping we wouldn't wake Kat.

I stared at Niki for a minute, at her long dark hair, her tight dress, her round full breasts, the shape of which were easily seen through the thin stretchy fabric of the dress. My eyes trailed down from the fullness on top to the curve of her hips and that sweet ass of hers pulled me to her like a damn magnet. I couldn't suppress the growl that erupted from my throat like I was some kind of goddamn animal.

I walked up behind her and seized her by the hips, drawing her back against me. "Damn baby, you're so hot," I mouthed against the skin of her neck. I slid my arms around her and inhaled the warm floral scent of her hair. "I can't keep my hands off you. I need you near me like this, pressed against my body."

She made me hard in an instant and I wanted her

lying naked on the bed, moaning and writhing with desire under me, biting her lip and spreading her legs for me.

But tonight didn't call for going all 'caveman' on her. I wanted to go slow, slow and easy. Smooth out all the knots after an emotional day. I knew that the fervor brewing inside of her would make it even sweeter when she opened her legs to me, whimpering, 'Oh, Jesse…' begging for me to hold her, caress her. All of today's tension would be twisted up inside of her, mixed in with her lust and that kind of volatile cocktail of torqued up emotions always made for a fucking explosive release.

I nuzzled her hair. Electric vibrations buzzed across every inch of my skin. Just being close to her like this, kissing the side of her neck, caused it. She arched out and moaned.

"I want to feel your touch, all over me…"

She clasped my hand to her breast harder and I squeezed it. The fullness in my hand arced another jolt to my groin and I pinched her nipple with my thumb and finger through her dress. Fuck, I could feel it was already hard and budded up, even through her clothes. I bet she was wet for me too. Mmm, another pleasure jolt to the groin.

My hand wandered from her breasts down along the slope of her stomach. My dick was rock hard now and I really wanted to shove my tongue down her throat, but I was hungry to feel the pressure of her ass on my cock a little longer. I had to push my hand against her pelvis so she would grind up against it. I couldn't wait much longer. The rush made me suck in air through my teeth and I pushed a couple of times, harder, grinding her into me. I whispered in her ear, "Feel this, Niki? This is how hard you make me." She practically purred and wiggled her backside up against me even more. My hands continued down to the edge of her dress and I slowly tugged it upward in a gradual reveal of her body.

Damn, she was fine as wine in nothing but her matching black lace bra and panties. I groaned silently, and cupped her breasts from behind. I looked down at her and all I wanted was to tear her panties off and get busy. Instead, I released the clasp of her bra and let it fall to the floor. She closed her eyes and inhaled, tipping her head back against mine. I felt the heat of her naked body against me. I wanted to rip my clothes off but I refrained, which was incredibly difficult to do since she was practically naked in my arms.

But I wanted to take it slow.

Painfully slow.

She put her hands on top of mine, stroked my arms, pressed me to her warm smooth skin as I caressed her tits. I ached for her tits. They were magnificently soft and round and her nipples were budded up to the sky. I kissed her neck, her smooth back, down to her waist, and bent down on one knee behind her, tracing her soft skin under my fingertips as I went. I reached around and pulled her toward me, pressing the palm of my hand on her stomach.

Touching her like this set me on fire. Every. Damn. Time.

I gently pulled down her lace panties and pressed my nose to the top of her rump. Her flesh there was soft and I kissed it. All over.

I caught a sweet whiff of her feminine scent and it made me lick my lips. She trembled. I felt it. She inhaled a quick gasp and I heard it. I knew she had to open her mouth to do that and my cock jerked harder at the thought of it.

I slid my hand down and grabbed her ankle. She bent the knee of that leg to release her panties and they fell to the floor. I slid my hands up both of her legs, up until they reach the softness of her thighs, and smoothed my palms over her round ass cheeks. I gently nudged the inside of her legs for her to step wider, and she complied. I had both of my hands on her ass, kneading with each thumb, working inward with each push, inch by inch, closer and closer to her wetness. She whimpered. *Fuck.* She's so wet now, warm and soft. I gulped and fought the urge to grab her and bury myself in her right now. But I wanted her to realize it wasn't just all about the sex with her. She was the only girl that had made me want to change.

I easily slid my finger inside of her, rubbing and stroking. My fingers moved fluidly and she inhaled, her breath shaking.

"Jesse…" she whispered.

"Do you want me to stop?" *Please say no, please say no, please say no.*

"No."

I got my wish and I breathed again.

"I love you inside of me, every part of you," she said in a soft voice.

I sucked in a breath and pushed my fingers in again, sliding in and out, up and around her hot little nub, giving her just a taste of what was to come, getting her all wound up so once I got her on the bed, all spread eagle and wet, begging, 'please Jesse, please,' she would make that high pitched girl sound that was so fucking hot. That sound triggered things in me. Things I didn't understand, animalistic kinds of reactions that seemed to come from who the hell knew where. But it's so…fucking…hot.

I stood and turned her to face me, loving the sight of her in front of me, wanting to please her endlessly. Slowly, gently, I used my entire body to edge her back toward the bed. I groaned and dropped my head, kissing her as we moved back.

She slid her hands between us, clawing at my T-shirt. I tore it off and tossed it aside but I wanted her to undo my black jeans. I wanted her fingers working me over. I wanted to look down and see her head near my crotch as she teased the zipper down. Any time a guy sees a woman's head near his crotch, that's just damn fucking hot.

I stroked my tongue across the exposed curve of her

breasts. "I want you," she said, breathless, the air from her words puffing in my hair. I lowered her gently back against the bed and eased down on top of her. I ran my tongue up the length of her neck and kissed her again, hard and deep. She plunged her tongue in my mouth and she tasted as sweet as ever. It caused my gut to clench and made me hard as hell. I wanted her legs wrapped around my hips. I wanted to drive it in deep and hard, but I was going easy tonight. Soft and slow. Savoring each lick of her plump lips, each smooth curve of her body. I had thoughts of doing this to her every day, when I woke up, when I went to sleep - especially when I went to sleep. I had thoughts of wrapping my arms around her gorgeous nakedness and fucking her, soft and slow, every minute of every day.

A strand of her dark brown hair lay across her cheek. I smoothed it aside with the palm of my hand, pushing it back, feeling the shape of her face under my fingers, so tender and delicate. Her eyes fluttered a little and she looked at me with half open eyes. Something welled up inside of my chest. I had a fierce feeling to protect her, always protect her. Kissing her again I felt desperation, a kind of fervent need, that could keep me in her arms forever. I could taste this girl every day and still never have enough.

I kissed her neck, her shoulder, all the way to her delicious breasts. I caressed them, and rubbed the bud of her nipples with my thumbs, winding her up into a highly aroused state. Her moans were fucking hot. They made me suck her nipples into my mouth and lick them harder. My blood was on fire for this girl and my balls were aching. I desperately needed more of her.

I held her gaze and coasted my fingertips across the sensitive skin of her thighs. I trailed higher, between her legs, stroking and teasing her most tender areas. Her body jerked in response to the first touch and she cried out desperately. It made me smile. I liked to see the pleasure I gave her in her eyes. I leaned my body over hers and pinned her down with another kiss. I felt her give in and submit to the pleasure even more. I could feel it in her muscles, she was riding the wave of an orgasm already, panting and twisting under me. And I had done nothing but touch her little sweet spot.

"You like that, baby?" My voice came out raspy, my vocal chords heavily laden with testosterone.

"Yes…" she whimpered and her body bucked in reaction to the intense strokes of my fingertips. I slipped and slid my fingers in her wetness, but I had to finish her off tasting that wetness. Then after I was done fucking her with my tongue, I could fuck her soft and slow with my cock.

I kissed her softly; each slow kiss enhanced the bolts of pleasure that flooded my already raw nerves. She moaned against my mouth and I caressed her tongue, coaxing her into another kiss. My body moved with hers as my fingers did their work. I swear I could feel her heartbeat, pounding against my chest. It was a turn on, giving her pleasure, watching her move. It aroused me and would later push my orgasm to greater heights. She was wound up tight as a spring right now so I dipped down, to taste her, to use my tongue to take her over the edge. A deep pleasurable moan erupted from her lips and I knew she had crested and come.

She had curled her body up and grabbed my hair when she climaxed. I was breathing heavily when I lifted my head and I had to take a second to adore the sight. Her body was so beautiful and her eyes were burning with desire. With our gaze locked, she lay back down against the bed and I entered her slowly, controlling myself to be gentle and easy this time. Her wetness made my penetration glide in readily, stretching her, filling her, satisfying her need to feel me inside of her.

"Jesse..." she whispered my name. My body jerked and my hips jutted against hers like a race horse wanting to jump the line. But I calmed myself.

I breathed out then inhaled, a long steady breath, through my nose, buried in her hair against the pillow. Our bodies moved slowly, rhythmically. She responded to each of my thrusts, the two of us moving together in synchronicity, her matching my pace. I knew the rhythm that would please her, the rhythm that would show her a different side of me. To show her with my body what I couldn't put into words, what I couldn't say out loud. The room filled with soft gasps and murmurs of pleasure, each other's names cried out in the heat of passion, all music to the soul.

Each breath was like another note, warm and soft, resonating inside of me all the way to my toes. I grasped her hips firmly and angled her so that I could stroke deeply inside of her. My rapid thrusts were matched by her cries of pleasure and I rocked my hips until I exploded and came inside of her. I kissed her panting lips one more time and rolled off of her, both of us spent, and collapsed onto the bed beside her.

Niki stared at me now, caressing me with her green eyes. Eyes like none I had ever seen before. Sexy and yet full of, full of…something very special that works its way inside of me every time she looks at me like this, all cuddled up in my arms, her skin pressed to mine, looking up with a little satisfied smile. It's like she can look right inside of me. And when she gives me that look, it does unexplainable things to me; marvelous and magical contortions twirl around inside my body.

No other girl had ever had this effect on me and it seemed to have arrived completely unexpected the night I first saw her. *Fuck me.* I was caught totally off guard. The air seemed to whoosh right out of me and it felt like I'd been hit with a two by four…but in a good way.

I was surprised at how I was changing. Niki made me want to be a better person. My behavior pattern in the past was pretty much 'let the hormones do the talking and my body to the walking.' It was easier to drown my sorrows and be a man-whore than deal with life's problems. *Oh, fuck me twice.* I was pussy-whipped. That's okay, all I knew was...Niki was so fucking beautiful; she was everything I was not and it blew my mind that she hadn't told me to go pound sand.

I smiled down at her. She seemed as drawn to me as I was to her. Or at least I hoped she was if, I was reading all these googly-eyed moments right. I wanted to do every fucking thing with this woman, and *for* this woman. It had been a long time since I'd put myself out there...there was no turning back now. I just hoped that she wouldn't stomp on my heart and leave me crying like a whiny little bitch.

Niki's petite hand had gone limp as it rested on my chest. She was asleep. I tucked her body up, close to mine, and let my eyelids drag shut with a huge mother fucking smile on my face.

CHAPTER 8

Niki

The clink of silverware on plates rattled me out of my sleep the next morning. The breakfast sounds of Kat poking around in the kitchen were loud enough to wake the dead as they passed through the walls of our apartment, right into my bedroom, right into my ear, which was pressed against the bare skin of Jesse's shoulder. I glanced at my alarm clock. It was only eight in the morning. Why the heck would Kat be up this early on a Sunday?

I wiggled out from underneath the muscles of his firm body and slipped out of bed. He was sleeping heavily, tired from last night's performance, no doubt, and what a performance it had been! Remembering the details brought a crooked smile to my face. He was so handsome, lying there naked, with the sheet covering only the left half of his magnificent body. I leaned down and lightly traced a finger across his tattoo, tempted to sneak back into bed and wake up my man for a repeat of last night. But my curiosity about what was going on in the kitchen got the better of me. And I figured he deserved to rest, after the ill treatment he'd had to put up with at my dad's house.

I picked up my robe and hurried out of the bedroom to see what the fuss was all about. As I tiptoed into the kitchen, Kat stood, in a tank top and pajama shorts, looking out the window.

"Morning!"

Kat nearly dropped her coffee mug. "Niki," she gasped. She checked the kitchen clock. No doubt she was wondering why I was up at this hour on a Sunday too. Kat was my best friend and if something was wrong I wanted to help.

"Sorry, didn't mean to startle you," I said, as I grabbed a cup from the cupboard and poured some coffee. "What are you doing up so early?"

"I feel like shit. Just spent the last fifteen minutes puking up last night's dinner." She pulled her feet up onto the seat of the chair and wrapped her arms around her knees, still holding the mug.

I choked on my coffee. "Shit! You are not pregnant are you?" I wrinkled my nose. I had forgotten to add cream and sugar, I was so engrossed in Kat's situation.

"You're shitting me, right? Me, pregnant? You're the only one in this household getting any action lately. And judging from that smile plastered on your face, I guess all that screaming last night was genuine," she chuckled.

I lightly slapped her shoulder. "Shut up, girl! But yeah. I'm not gonna lie. It was pretty fantastic. So why were you puking?"

"I don't know. Guess it was something I ate…or drank…or both. I feel a little better, now that most of last night's dinner has gone down the toilet." She let one leg down and sat with the other still bent up on the chair. Kat took a sip of her coffee. "So how did it go at your dad's?"

"Oh, you don't wanna know." I added creamer and sweetener.

"Oh, but I *do*. You promised me all the juicy details."

I slowly swirled the spoon in the light brown liquid. "I don't know. Nothing much happened." I pulled the spoon out, licked it and held it like a popsicle with one arm folded across my body. "Let's see, besides my evil stepmom eye-fucking my boyfriend, and listening to my dad's spiteful remarks about how much of a loser Jesse is and how he could never compare to Jason…not much excitement."

Kat nodded. "Why am I not surprised? Sounds like what I imagined would happen. He's the parent. It's his job to make you feel like you're wrong. The only reason he likes Jason is because he is his pick, he's in control that way, but in reality, nobody's good enough for his little girl. But go on."

"Oh yeah, the highlight of the night was when Jesse threatened to break Jason's nose if he continues stalking me. It sent Jason running for the hills." I snorted a laugh. "But besides that, nothing much else.

Except that I am probably going to be penniless after the things I said to my dad. I even sort of hit him."

"You did what! Did you punch him?"

"No, no, I just shoved him, like this." I put my palms up and pushed at the air. "...on his chest."

"That is so kickass..."

"I was so angry. He knows exactly how to get me upset, knows just the right words to send me into a rage. I was pissed; no, I was more than pissed."

"Like, what did he say?"

"He insulted my mom, and you know how defensive I am about her."

"Fuck, Niki. That's low. But I'm happy for you that you're finally standing up for yourself with your dad. I bet it's been a long time since he last saw such fearless fighter spirit in you."

"I guess not since I was a kid."

"I know you've mentioned your mom a little but, you've never told me what really happened, back when she died. In fact, you've never told me much about her at all." Kat seemed to be picking her words carefully. She didn't want to pry and open old wounds.

She was right. I never liked to talk about it. Partly because I always blamed myself for what happened. It was a dark time and something I just wanted to put aside. Opening up to Kat, or anyone else for that matter, and Jesse especially, wasn't easy for me. But harboring secrets was emotionally exhausting and I was getting really tired of it.

"I know. I only remember a few things from before she got sick, but I protect those memories with all I have. It's like they are delicate and brittle and, if I don't guard them, they might disappear someday, crumble and turn to dust. I know that's why I overreact whenever my dad says anything negative about her." I rubbed at a brown coffee stain on the white tile countertop with my thumb. "After she died, I went through a very emotional time. There aren't many good memories from that part of my life. I wish those memories would go away, but they don't. They get all mixed up with my relationship with my dad, you know? So I like to leave it at that. If I don't talk about the bad memories, maybe they'll finally go away."

Kat nodded. She got it. She was good at knowing when to let a subject rest and when to lighten the mood. "Well, enough of that. So what's on your calendar for today, Miss Erotic Goddess? More bedroom fitness with Casanova boy?"

I shot her a devilish glance and wiggled my eyebrows. "Maybe I should go wake him."

"Yeah right. Let me get out of the house first. All the moaning and groaning makes a girl horny. I'll end up joining you guys."

"Oh yeah?" I chuckled. "Sorry, hun. Not into threesomes today, although I'm sure Jesse would enjoy that." I laughed and tiptoed back into the bedroom before Kat got any more ideas about sharing.

Jesse was still asleep. I crawled under the sheet,

scooting as close to him as I could get. My hands traveled down his tight stomach, all the way down. He was naked, his cock half erect. I wrapped my hand around it and started slowly stroking up and down. It stiffened. He woke slightly and repositioned himself to allow me easier access. Although his eyes were closed, a sexy smile curved up his lips, betraying his conscious state. As he moved, the sheet slipped away and I nearly gasped at the sight of his nakedness. He rolled toward me, slipped his hand around my neck, kissed my lips lightly and then my cheek, murmuring a pleasurable sound. "Mmmm, good morning, beautiful."

Beautiful was hardly the word for my messed up morning hair and I'd forgotten to check the mirror to see if I had mascara smudges under my eyes. Before a single protest could make it to my lips, Jesse smothered them with his own and my body naturally curved toward his. I sighed with contentment as his hand trailed down along the slope of my neck and across my collarbone. The warmth of his palm brushed my nipple, as his hand cupped each breast and teased it, while he deepened our kiss. I throbbed with need by the time he pulled away from me and he opened his smoldering blue eyes. He brushed my hair back from my face and lowered himself to take one of my breasts into his mouth. I shivered at the sudden wetness, and threw my head back with pleasure. I ran my hand over the strong rise of his shoulders, down along his shoulder blades. His hands pushed my knees apart and he slid down farther, switching his attention to my other breast. I savored each subtle touch of his lips and tongue and swirled my fingers through his hair. His fingertips slid between my folds and roamed along my sensitive nub.

"Jesse," I gasped out, as my body reacted to his touch.

"Yes?" he murmured, as he kissed from my breast up to the base of my neck.

"Are you trying to seduce me?" I asked and squirmed at his insistent touch.

"Oh yes," he replied and pressed his lips to mine. When he broke the kiss he eyed me mischievously.

"Is it working?" He arched a brow.

"You really need to ask?" I replied opening my legs further in a submissive gesture. He continued to tease me with his fingers as his lips roamed from breast to breast, and back to my lips again. His lips wandered down over the slope of my stomach. As he moved down, millions of pleasure tingles jetted up. I closed my eyes and sucked in a breath in anticipation and was rewarded with the warmth of his tongue, languidly caressing my hot spot.

A rush of blood ripped through my body, so intense that I fisted my hands into the sheets as if that could steady the passion that rocked me. The sudden tension jerked my body, as a signal for him to continue, and a deep moan escaped my lips. He eased my legs up, over each of his shoulders, and continued to flick and swirl his tongue as I squirmed and bucked on the bed.

"Oh Jesse," I gasped out. My body shook and convulsed. I moaned aloud with erotic pleasure as my whole being flooded with ecstasy. I abandoned myself to the whirl of sensations pulsing through my body and the next moan was accompanied by the rush of my orgasm. Panting breathlessly, he rose up and caught each of my legs behind the knee and pushed them up, until my knees were almost to my ears. Jesse was an animal. I was a little startled, as it was quite different from last night's smooth as Barry White love making. Whether he was Easy Breezy Jesse or Hurricane Harbor Jesse, either way, that's the way I liked it.

From the size of his rock hard erection, I could tell his body still craved mine and he thrust deep inside of me, ready for his turn.

"Fuck me, baby, fuck me. I'm all yours," I gasped.

A satisfied growl tore from deep within his throat. With each thrust, he groaned louder, gripping the backs of my thighs, driving deeper with each penetration. Euphoric screams burst forth from my lips, surprising even me, and were met with equally intense growls from Jesse.

I managed to part my eyes long enough to catch a glimpse of Jesse's expression and I was stunned by it. With his eyes squeezed shut, his lips spread apart and greedily searching for air, a hot tide of passion raged through him, and he shuddered and climaxed inside of me. Even as we both wound down from the heady pleasure of our experience, our lips and touches sought and explored each other's bodies.

As I unfurled from his grasp, I smirked. "We better get out of bed now, or we never will." I laughed.

Jesse pretended to pout. "What's so wrong with that?" he asked, and grabbed playfully at my ankle as I started to crawl away.

I sheepishly poked my head out of the bedroom, listening for sounds of Kat. Thank God she had escaped the building—or more like she had escaped the torture of listening to our lust filled moans and screams—and I avoided an awkward roommate moment.

"Are you hungry?" I asked.

"Starving. Wanna go out for breakfast?"

"I can fix you some eggs and bacon if you like?"

Jesse sneaked up behind me and placed his hands on my hips. "Depends. Are you a good cook?" he teased.

"Only one way to find out! But seriously, who can mess up bacon and eggs?"

"You haven't tasted *my* cooking. Trust me. I can mess up eggs and bacon."

I laughed and swatted his firm butt. "Well, get out of my way so I can cook for my man."

He pulled out a chair, sat down and watched me crack four eggs. "Sunny side up?"

"Sure, however you like them."

"Perfect, I like a guy who's not picky about food."

Soon we were sitting across from each other, in my little kitchen, feeling very homey. It felt good to have

Jesse with me like this. Jesse had worked up quite an appetite and it didn't take him more than a couple of minutes to finish his food. He pushed his plate away and steepled his fingers under his chin.

"By the way, Niki. I was going to ask you last night but got a little... sidetracked." He winked. "You know your friend I met at the bonfire, Jenna? She's a journalist, right?"

"Yeah. Well, sort of. She works at the L.A. Times. She's not really a journalist yet. Why?" I finished and placed my knife and fork neatly on the plate.

"You know Kenny's bar isn't doing too well financially. You've been in there lately. You've seen how empty it is. I feel like I'm letting Kenny down. He's wrapped up with his cancer treatments, and Chase and I are in charge, and the damn place is going downhill. I'm just brainstorming ways to boost business. I don't know shit about marketing but maybe Jenna could get us a good deal on a newspaper ad. Promote the place a little."

"I doubt it. The L.A. Times is expensive and I'm not sure how much exposure it would bring. A better idea would be if we could have them do an article about Rookies. That would be free promotion."

"A story about a sports bar? There are hundreds of bars like that in L.A."

"None of them have a hot, super star, Motocross rider serving drinks behind the bar. Besides..." I tapped my finger on the table top for emphasis. "There's a real story here about you and Kenny - the bone marrow transplant and everything. You're a true to life hero, Jesse."

The thought popped into my mind and made me feel happy. Jesse was the real thing, almost too good to be true. He made my heart race. I couldn't believe he was mine. I couldn't believe my life was... I glanced down at the yolk stain on the plate, well, sunny side up, like the eggs this morning. I had been blindsided by my own issues, so caught up in my own defenses, I'd nearly lost out on the best thing to ever happen in my life. I searched his dark blue eyes, waiting for his reaction to my idea.

"I don't know about that." He laughed and leaned back in his chair. "I'm no freaking hero, but I'm glad *you* think so."

"Will you do it?"

He pursed his lips, tilted his head and gave me a sidelong glance. "Sure, why not. As long as the emphasis is on the *bar* and not me."

I jumped up and leaned across the table and planted a big wet kiss on his lips. "Thank you, baby." I walked over and tipped my plate into the sink. "I can't promise anything about the focus of their piece. They'll write whatever is the best story for their readers. But as far as the bar is concerned, it's better than nothing."

"Alright, cool. Can you set it up…call Jenna?"

"I will, baby. I will do anything for you." I batted my lashes theatrically, with my fingers laced under my chin like a Southern Belle.

He rose from the table, handing me his plate and played along. "Anything? Hmm...I can think of something."

A wicked smile grew across his face as he walked towards me. I laughed, picked up the dish towel and threw it at him.

"Down boy," I teased. He leaned to the side and easily dodged my poor aim, letting the towel fall to the floor.

"You said anything."

I braced myself like I was ready to run, but I was joshing. I had no intention of running from Jesse, ever again. He stepped closer and I let him catch me in his strong arms. Circling them around me, he pulled me close to the firm, tight muscles of his chest. He dipped his head down to me, grazing the outer edge of my ear lightly, playfully, with his nose, his hot breath fanning me all the way down my neck. I felt the wetness of his mouth as he tugged my earlobe with his teeth. My body melted into his firm frame and a hot shudder coursed through me. As my lips parted for his kiss I murmured, "I did, didn't I?"

He crushed his mouth against mine. Tingles of anticipation reared up again, for the second time that morning, and it surprised me. He filled my whole being with wanting. I didn't think I could ever get enough of Jesse Morrison.

CHAPTER 9

Jesse

"Hey, Jesse, can I talk with you for a second?" A faint knock came from the other side of the bedroom door.

"Sure...*Pops*." I said in a sarcastic voice. "Come on in. It's your house." I tossed my Motocross magazine across the room and it landed neatly on the table.

Kenny pushed the door open. "Jesus, how long are you going to torment me about this Dad thing?"

"Just long enough for you to tell me the truth."

"I told you everything I goddamn know. What else do you want to hear?"

"Maybe the real reason why you left us, after Dad died. And don't give me that bullshit about Mom demanding you leave. That doesn't fly with me. I know she had feelings for you."

"I don't know what else to say, Jesse," his voice rose in pitch and he exhaled. "Ask her yourself. I'm sure she had her reasons." He rubbed the back of his neck and held onto the door knob with the other hand. From the expression on his face I could see Kenny had a bug up his ass; there was something else on his mind and he wasn't in the mood to listen to my whiny rant. The sad look on his face made me check my attitude with him and I kicked up and sat on the edge of the bed.

"Whatever…anyway, what is it?" I sighed, leaned my elbows on my knees, and rubbed my face with my hands.

"I was going over last week's accounts and the income from sales at the bar is down more than fifty percent. What the hell are you and Chase doing? Sitting around with your thumbs up your asses?"

"You make it sound like it's *our* fault. We're trying hard to attract customers. I've never owned a business. I don't know what the hell to do and you're not there to help…" The tension was getting to all of us lately, causing us to snap at each other. I was under pressure to help Kenny, Chase was afraid he'd lose his job and Kenny was – well - fucked.

It felt like I had the weight of the world on my shoulders, but before I could speak again, Kenny cut me off. "You're not the one who has cancer, puking the living shit out of yourself every day." He was turning beet red and I thought he might stroke-out on the floor at any minute.

I stood up and took a step toward Kenny, in case he passed out or something. Shit, I didn't know much about what his cancer treatment did, but it sure made him sick.

"Hey, Kenny, you want to sit down?" I peered into his face. He was breathing hard but in a couple seconds his breaths slowed to normal. "Sorry to snap at you, we are all on edge here, these days. Let's slow down and take it easy." He nodded. "Come on, you need some water? Let's go to the kitchen. I could use a drink, but I'll settle for water."

Kenny managed a meek smile at my bad joke and we moved our conversation to the kitchen

"So what exactly are you talking about? What are you doing to attract customers?"

"Well, it so happens that *maybe*, we can get an article about Rookies in the L.A. Times. That should attract some customers."

"Forgive me if I don't pat you on the back, but how'd you manage that?" He looked at me like I was full of shit.

"It was Niki's idea. She knows someone who works for the newspaper and dropped a hint or two. I'm waiting to hear back, from the journalist assigned to the article, with a time and a place for the interview."

"Place? Won't the interview be at the bar?"

"I hope so. That's what I suggested. But they want the focus of the article to be on me, the motocross champ who came from New York to help out his ailing uncle and help save his bar from closing. Kind of a sappy, pathetic story if you ask me." My mouth inched into a crooked smile.

Kenny snorted a laugh. "That *is* pathetic." He pulled

out a chair, sat down at the kitchen table, and put his head in his hands. "Seriously, that is the best thing anyone has ever done for me. And to think that you came from *my* sorry ass genes." He shook his head.

"I'm psyched about it. Anything for the cause…"

"It's a fucking miracle…" His voice choked off the rest of his words and he ran the back of his hand across his cheek.

"Hey, man. Don't get all mushy on me. You would've done the same for me. In fact, you did, back when I was a kid." I moved toward Kenny and wrapped my arms around him in a bear hug.

"I'm okay." He huffed and swatted me away. "So how is that hand of yours coming along? Feeling any better?"

I opened and closed my hand into a tight fist. "It's getting a lot better. I'm itching to get back on a bike. It's killing me that I haven't been able to ride. My bike is in storage, back home."

I noticed Kenny's face light up. "Jess, you're in luck. I have an old Harley you can borrow, if you want. I know it's not a dirt bike and it needs a little TLC but it should still run. It might relieve the itch."

"No fucking way. A Harley? Which series?"

"A Fatboy, big twin-engine, you know, the one with the large telescopic fork upfront, makes it look like a chopper from the 1960s."

"Where the hell did you hide that?"

"It's out back, in that rickety looking shed. Come on.

Let's take a look at it."

"Fuck yeah." We left the kitchen and I followed Kenny out to what I thought was a shed for his lawn mower and yard stuff.

"You know how the Fatboy got its name, don't you?" He slid open the back patio door. "Rumor has it that the name was made up of a combination of the nicknames that were given to the two atomic bombs dropped on Nagasaki and Hiroshima: Fat Man and Little Boy."

"No way…"

"Well, it's an urban legend, anyway."

It was just like old times again, Kenny schooling me on the knowledge of motorcycles; only this time it wasn't as my uncle but as my dad.

Kenny twisted the key in the padlock and flipped it open, swinging wide the double doors of the shed. The front tire and a hint of shiny chrome peeked out from under a dusty black plastic cover, tailored to the fit the shape of the bike. He tilted his head in the direction of the bike. "Go ahead, pull the cover off."

He stood back and I removed the cover with a whoosh of dust.

"Wow, she's a beauty. Kenny, your bike is fucking bad ass!"

It looked to be a 1996 Fatboy, Harley-Davidson. It was beautiful; black with full chrome. It needed a little TLC, as Kenny said, but I couldn't wait to feel the ocean air hitting my face on a ride to Malibu.

"A little elbow grease should get it to run. The battery is probably dead after sitting for so long, but that's easy enough to fix. I might still have a battery charger in all this junk, but it's probably better just to buy a new one."

"Yeah, that old one might not hold a charge for long and I wouldn't want to get stranded somewhere out on the Pacific Coast Highway." I ran the palm of my hand along the smooth curve of the black high gloss gas tank, admiring its design. "And you are sure I can ride it?"

"It's the least I can do. I won't be riding it for quite a while. You think you can fix it up?"

"Absolutely...I learned from the best. It looks to be in pretty good shape."

"She's all yours. I gotta go lie down for a minute. I feel the nausea coming back."

"Okay, man. You need some help?"

"I'm good. Catch you later. Be sure to let me know when you set up that interview." He left and I turned to take a closer look at the beauty sitting in front of me. Fuck, she was sweet.

CHAPTER 10

Niki

Jenna had just called to let me know that they were going to run the article in Sunday's paper and I was giddy with excitement. Jesse would be so pleased. Apparently the editor loved the story so much it was set to be the featured article in the *Life and Health* section. I wanted to tell him in person so I texted him to invite him for lunch and some afternoon fun. Thursday was my short day of classes at school and Jesse had already arranged for Chase to cover for him at Rookies.

He immediately texted back:

"I was just about to text you, babe! I have a surprise. I'm taking you to Malibu. Wear jeans and no sandals. XOXO"

Jeans, no sandals? Highly unusual for a hot summer day. He had never told me what to wear before, but I would've worn a winter coat for Jesse if he'd asked me. With one quick jerk I flung off my summer dress and changed into a top and jeans.

Ten minutes later I got another text:

"I'm here. Meet me downstairs."

My curiosity was piqued by all this mystery and I was excited to spend the afternoon with Jesse. I skipped down the stairs. When I landed outside I pulled up short as I approached the parking lot.

You've gotta be kidding me.

I expected to be greeted by Jesse's huge truck, but instead he was sitting, with his legs spread, straddling the seat of a huge motorcycle. He looked sharp; no, hot. Damn hot in black jeans and black shirt. He wore dark leather gloves with a cut-out on the back side and as he pulled off the helmet, long stray locks of hair fell in his eyes. I walked the rest of the way to the bike with a huge grin on my face. Motorcycles just exuded the words 'bad boy' and as I approached a shiver went down my spine. I had actually never ridden on a motorcycle before.

"Where did you get *this*?" I admired its glistening chrome, sparkling in the sun. I supposed chrome, for men, was the equivalent of what bling was for women. *Big boys and their big toys.*

"Isn't it badass?" He flipped down the kickstand and swung one leg wide to dismount. "It's Kenny's. He's letting me borrow it. Crazy, I know. The cancer must have gotten to his brain," he said with a smile.

"Jesse, that's terrible. Chemo is not something to joke about."

"Ah, I don't mean it. He'll be fine. In fact, when this is over, he'll be better than new. He *is* getting my awesome bone marrow, you know."

He slipped an arm around my waist and brushed his lips against mine.

"Are you sure it's only your bone marrow he'll get with the transplant, and not your *cocky* attitude, too?" I teased.

Jesse's steel blue eyes danced under his dark brow; his lips curved, as if the question gave him mischievous ideas, and he shrugged.

He removed an old, scratched helmet that had been secured to the backrest with a bungee rope and held it out for me. "Come on, girl. Let's blow this Popsicle stand. Jump aboard. You get the 'bitch seat.' He nodded to the back seat, behind his.

I tucked my chin in and looked up at him like, 'oh no you didn't.'

"Okay, but if I turn into a royal biatch while sitting there, don't blame me."

He smiled and opened the chin straps to help me with helmet. "Hold on…" I dug in my purse for a pony holder. I'd seen girls on the back of motorcycles, with their hair flying all crazy in the wind, whipping it into a million split ends. I tied mine into a low ponytail and slung the long strap of my purse diagonally across my body. Jesse helped me as I slid the helmet on my head, fastening the chin strap for me as if I were a little child.

"There you go, baby." He stepped back and gave me the once over. "Ouw, mamma! You look like a hard core, bad ass chick in that helmet!"

"Yeah right. I'll make believe that's true for like two more seconds." I waved him away and wagged my head, side to side, testing out the feel of it. I was unaccustomed to the heavy weight of the helmet and I imagined I must have looked like one of those bobble-head figurines as I moved to mount the bike.

"Let me get on first and start it up, then you can hop on." He pushed his hair back with his hand and slipped on his helmet with the ease of someone who had done it a hundred times before. It struck me that he *was* a professional, very well-known for his sport, almost like a movie star. His machismo was staggering as he slung one leg over the seat and gripped the handlebars.

A spike of nervous energy passed through me, partially from fear of the unknown and partially from the goose bumps Jesse gave me. And okay, maybe I was a little excited to do something out of my comfort zone.

"I don't know. I have never ridden a bike before."

I am such a whiney bitch.

Oh God. I'm not even on it and the damn seat is already earning its name.

"Come on. It'll be great. Just hold on to me." Another rush of energy as he turned the key in the ignition and the beast rumbled to life. "Trust me. You're with an expert, baby."

I swallowed the moisture in my mouth. "Promise me you won't do anything dangerous."

"I promise. Now, get on the bike!"

Yikes! I placed one hand on Jesse's shoulder to anchor myself and stepped my left foot on the peg, swinging my other one up and over like I was mounting a horse. At least I had done *that* before. I could do this.

Equipped with the helmet, squashing my hair out of shape, we rode towards Pacific Coast Highway, which would take us to Malibu. It was exhilarating. I was astounded at how good it felt. It opened me up, just like Jesse. I was at a point in my life where I was stretching my limits, going for what I wanted, trusting my own gut and living life my way. Getting on the back of the motorcycle was just another avenue to push myself out of my comfort zone and be willing to be vulnerable.

The wind in my face felt refreshing and sitting there, with my arms around Jesse's firm and tight torso, made it even better. Every muscle on him was rock solid and sitting with my legs spread apart, so close behind him, I could feel and smell everything about him. All that, mixed with the mild engine vibrations I felt through the seat reverberating between my legs, made something hot and wild twitch in my core. Now I understood the allure of these machines. One big 'cock extension' for the guys and a very sensual experience for the girl riding in the…oh what the hell, the bitch seat.

"Not too bad, right?" Jesse asked, turning his head to the side and trying to out yell the wind.

"Hell, yes! It feels good."

The bike slowed as we approached a T-intersection with a red light.

"Watch this." Jesse snaked the bike in between two rows of cars, splitting lanes on the PCH, waiting for the light to turn green. When he pulled up to the line, we were positioned right next to a red convertible Ferrari.

A young, tan guy with tousled, Justin Bieber hair shouted from the Ferrari in Jesse's direction, "Nice ride!" His passenger sat next to him, with a stone face in dark sunglasses, looking dead ahead.

Jesse nodded and gave his thank you with a twist of the throttle and the engine revved. "Fuckin A!" Jesse called out and gave the 'shaka' hand gesture, a short shake of the hand with the pinky and thumb extended to the guy. I don't speak 'guy-talk' but I was pretty sure it meant, 'I like your Ferrari too, dude.' There was so much testosterone whipping in the wind, right there on the PCH, it could've been wrung out of the air.

I heard the taunting pitch of the Ferrari's V-12 engine as it whined, ramping up its revolutions. *Oh shit.* Justin Bieber just threw down a challenge.

"Think you can take me?" He called back with a, 'Hi, I'm young and stupid' smirk.

Jesse gave a quick pat to my left thigh and cranked down on the throttle again. "Any time, dude. You're toast."

And why does Jesse think this is a good idea? Panic entered my brain. So much for pushing my limits. I can't die today. I have an appointment to get my nails done tomorrow. "No, Jesse. Don't!" I screamed.

Jesse's helmet pointed straight ahead. No doubt he

had his eye trained on the traffic light. The two engines whirred and screamed as they spun up, waiting for the light to change. Jesse leaned slightly forward, gunning the Harley's unique twin engines, poised to slam it in first gear. He was fearless. The engines of the bike and the car roared back and forth to each other, like dueling pianos on steroids.

I was now sure my life was over. This was it. In a second, the light would change and I'd be dead or in a wheelchair for the rest of my life.

I squeezed my eyes shut tightly.

Oh shit.

Help me, Jesus.

Why can't I be more like Jesse and seize the day?

Before I knew it, the light turned green and the Ferrari blasted off the line, racing down the road with us cruising a mediocre forty-five mph behind. My heart was pounding out of my chest. Jesse didn't race. The taillights of the red Italian sports car were already out of sight.

I relaxed my death grip from around his waist and slumped forward against his back. "You scared the shit out of me. Why didn't you go?" I shouted so he could hear through the helmet.

Jesse shifted into high gear and sank back in his seat to cruise for several miles, one hand on the throttle and his left hand resting casually on his thigh. He turned his head to the left and shouted over the wind, "I'm not an idiot. There's no way a Harley can take a Ferrari. I was just messing with that guy."

I smiled. I chastised myself for distrusting Jesse. He might be impulsive and reckless when it came to bar fights, but I was glad to learn he wasn't that way with me.

The PCH was a beautiful stretch of winding highway that led up the Coast of California. It was a perfect scenic route to enjoy, on a warm day, with the jagged ocean cliffs and cresting waves completely in open view from the backseat of a motorcycle. Breathtakingly beautiful. Jesse reached back with his left hand and stroked my thigh, wedged up against his side. His large hand easily palmed the top of my knee and he stroked up and down my jean covered leg, his thumb nearly reaching all the way up between my legs on the up stroke. Bitch seat my ass...this was more like a massage with a happy ending.

No sooner had we pulled out of a sharp bend in the road when we caught sight of a sports car, pulled over on the side of the road. It was none other than Justin Bieber and his red Ferrari, alongside a California Highway Patrol motorcycle cop. The CHP officer had probably been waiting just around the bend, with his radar gun pointed at oncoming traffic. That was their usual M.O. I had seen it numerous times before on California streets and highways. Jesse waved at the driver as we passed, traveling at a smooth sixty miles an hour.

Jesse turned his head again to shout back to me,

"Baby, you're my guardian angel. I would've given that guy a run for his money if you hadn't have been here."

I pulled my arms tighter around Jesse's waist, enjoying every moment. The craggy, creaking sound of the steel doors to my heart could practically be heard above the wind blasting past us, as they opened a little more. I had never felt this free and happy before.

We stopped at a cute little Italian restaurant called Mi Piazzi on the PCH, just outside Malibu. As we entered we were greeted by an elderly host, who looked as if he had just got off the boat from Italy.

"Buongiorno. I have just the perfect table for you two." His accent was thick and absolutely authentic. I took Jesse's hand as we were led through the restaurant to our table, on the patio with an ocean view. The sound of squawking seagulls filtered through the air as I watched them dive and peck at people's lunches, down on the beach, below. The crash of the waves, the sand, being on a motorcycle adventure with Jesse - what could be more romantic?

Jesse stared at me intently. The expression on his handsome face was pure satisfaction after his motorcycle ride. He told me it was his first real experience back on a bike after his injury, other than taking the bike for a test drive after he fixed it. My belly twinged as I stared back at him, and the hope in his eyes swirled into future possibilities of many more days with me on the back of a bike. Phrases like, 'motorcycle mamma' and 'his old biker lady' sprang, with horror, into my mind. Eeww! That wasn't my self-image; but it tickled me nonetheless, as a humorous juxtaposition against my stylish fashion design persona.

Scolding myself for being so quick to judge, I entertained the idea of donning a tube top and black leather chaps. Getting really tan to show off my abs, so Jesse would drool over me in super low rise jeans that curved just right over the rise of my ass. It could happen. I reconsidered as I pictured myself wearing lots of silver studded black leather. I could rock that look.

I swallowed hard, coming back to myself, wondering if Jesse noticed my little flight of fantasy. I touched my hand lightly to my throat and blinked, redirecting my attention to Jesse's voice.

"I love this restaurant. It reminds me of a little tavern I used to dine at when I was in Italy last year."

Italy? Now that sounded super romantic.

"How long were you there?"

"A week. We had a few extra days between races so I stayed longer than normal. It was like a mini vacation. I can't wait to go back."

"It must be amazing, traveling the world and getting paid for it," I said.

"You would think so, but most of the time you don't see much, except for airports, hotel rooms and the track. It's really not all it's cracked up to be. I don't do it for the travelling, sightseeing, or even the money. Racing is in my blood. I live for it. No matter how bad my day has been, when I get on that bike, my day is instantly so much better." He leaned back in his chair and folded his arms across his chest. "That's why it was so frustrating for me to be injured," he said casting his gaze towards the ocean view.

"Which do you like to race better, Supercross or Motocross? I mean, I don't really know the difference."

"Well, basically, Supercross was an offshoot of Motocross, it's very similar in many ways. Like, Supercross tracks are more technical and not as fast as Motocross tracks, but with higher difficulty levels. And that adds to the risk of injuries, hence…" He held up his hand that had been injured and wiggled his fingers.

"When do you think you will be ready to race again?"

His eyes caught mine and he smiled. "It will be a while. First, I have to get back in shape. Get all the alcohol out of my system," he chuckled. "I need several months of strength and endurance training. I *definitely* won't be ready for Supercross season. That starts in about four months, so I'll focus on Motocross, instead. The world championship doesn't start until spring next year…anyway, plenty of time to get ready for that."

The waiter brought us our appetizer, an antipasto salad with a selection of Italian meats and cheeses.

"This is delicious," I said, chewing on a piece of provolone with Italian salami.

"I could eat like this for the rest of my life and die happy."

"You are just full of surprises, Jesse. I had no idea you were such a foodie."

"It comes from being on the road in Europe. I got tired of burgers and pizza so, instead of having the same old stuff every day, I decided to try something new. Seize the day." He wiggled his eyebrows and cocked his right bicep forward.

"Carpe diem," we said simultaneously and laughed.

I stared down at my lap and I was suddenly overwhelmed with feelings of possessiveness. I didn't want anyone or anything to monopolize his time but me. I knew it was ridiculous to think such a thing, but it simply popped up. Unable to stop them, crazy, irrational feelings of jealousy flitted through my body. Thoughts of his job taking him back to New York gripped at my stomach uncomfortably and made me squirm in my chair.

I hadn't really anticipated this, him getting back into racing, or what it would entail. I had been so blinded by my desire for him that I had pushed those thoughts out of my mind, no - I hadn't even allowed them in my brain at all.

The day I went to his house, when Chase told me he was packing for New York, he agreed to stay and give us a chance; but I hadn't thought beyond that point in time. I hadn't contemplated the future. How stupid of me. To think he would give up his career, to stay in

California, for me. Helping Kenny at Rookies was a temporary gig. I knew that. *Stupid!* I could barely eat the antipasto salad on my plate. I picked at the slice of provolone, rolling and unrolling it with a slice of salami, but not eating it.

Jesse held my gaze across the table, his blazing blue eyes making me feel like I was the only woman there. Maybe I only saw what I wanted to see. Maybe his career was more than I could offer him; maybe it fulfilled him in a way I couldn't. Maybe I had been fooling myself but, for a few more minutes, I just wanted to sit in this dumb chair and believe that there could be a kind of magnetism between us, so alluring that it would solve everything.

A strange mix of anxiety and anticipation shot its way to the surface, like an angry Pit-bull, lunging to the end of its chain. Struggling with toxic emotions, I forced them back to speak.

"So, what are you going to do about training? I hope you don't have to go back to New York for that."

Jesse watched me, taunted me with a slow smile, checking for my reaction as he stared into my eyes. His gaze flitted to my plate, to my nervous twitchings with my food, and he took my hand away from it, pulling it into his, entwining our fingers as one. I shivered, though it was warm at the beach. Hairs prickled and my awareness shifted to the warm caress of his hand, his strong fingers working mine, rubbing, stroking, and sliding in and out between mine. I took him in; his long strands of hair, perfectly sexy strands, fell in an untamed fashion into those sapphire eyes.

They flickered to my lips and back to meet mine. He enveloped my hand in both of his and, leaning forward, drew them to his lips. I felt the fleshy softness of his mouth pressing on the back of my hand.

"I like to hear that from you."

A delicious buzz hummed through my bloodstream, while his gaze caught me and tamed me, like a wild Mustang. It was amazing what merely looking at this man did to my body. He untangled his fingers and lowered my hand to the table, leaving it hot and wet, like me. I blinked, and stared at the palm of my hand for a second, the fire of his kiss still burning like a freshly blazed tattoo, before I shoved it under the table.

"I can stay here for most of the training. There are plenty of facilities around L.A. I might have to do a longer stretch, at some point, at a training camp, once I join a team, but we'll see."

I felt my chest expand. My insides bubbled with emotions. I could breathe. We hadn't discussed how to handle the future, but it was a relief that we didn't have to make serious decisions about our relationship for a while.

I had a lot of pending issues with my family situation. After the birthday party fiasco, I felt like my life was in limbo, neither in Heaven nor Hell, just stuck, hanging in the middle in the vapors, wondering when and if my dad would cut me off financially.

Kat advised me to give my dad a day to cool down. I told her I'd maybe give him a month. My hot tempered dad didn't do 'cool.' Just a guess, but I don't think father-daughter relationships were covered in law school.

I patted myself on the back for making the progress I had: moving in with Kat, reinventing myself, just being in control of my own dreams in general. And then I met Jesse, the one man I was willing to trust with my heart, the first man who unnerved me with his good looks alone. Oh, he may have had a bad boy reputation, but he was sexier than sin and just when I was striking out on shaky trust legs, now he threw me for a loop with this talk of getting back into racing, which meant leaving me. Like the others. Like my mom. Like my dad. Was his passion for racing greater than his passion for me?

Melting into my chair, I could hardly get a word out. One weak little syllable managed to squeak its way out, past my inner turmoil, barely above a whisper. "Oh." I cleared my throat and tried to compose myself, as if none of it flustered me in the least. "What kind of team?"

"Last year I was with Yamaha, so I hope they'll take me back for next year's season. I have to go to New York in a couple weeks. I was... hoping you would come with me?" He ducked his head and peered up at me from under his dark lashes.

I exhaled and raised my eyebrows. "Phew, Jesse.

That's a tall order."

"You hesitated." He stared at me with uncertainty, pleading.

"I would love to, but I doubt I can afford a trip right now. My dad hasn't said a word to me since the birthday party. Who knows if he will even help me with rent anymore?"

His face lit up. "Don't worry about paying for the trip. I'll get the expense account to pay for you." His lip twitched. "Just give me a massage every night and we'll call you my personal physical therapist."

"Ha-ha. I can only imagine the kind of sessions you have in mind."

"Well, those are the bonus sessions. No, seriously, we can go see my brother too. It'll be a great trip. Are you in?"

"Maybe. I have to check my class schedule first."

"Come on, Niki. Come with me. It will be fun and I don't want to leave you here. I don't trust your dad. He might work a deal and have you in an arranged marriage by the time I get back." He joked but I could see there was a glimmer of anxiety in his eyes. He really wanted to be with me. It boosted my self-confidence to see it and I could feel my muscles relax. "It will be a couple of weeks until we leave, so you have time to figure out how to deal with your classes."

"It sounds wonderful, Jesse. But I'm going to pay for my own way, somehow, even if I have to pick up cans on the side of the road. I'll see what I can arrange."

My appetite reemerged, once I had turned down the crazy little voice of insecurity in my head. Everything was going to be okay. It reminded me of the good news I had yet to tell him. "Guess what is happening on Sunday?"

"What's on Sunday? The Dodgers game?"

"No, silly. Before you picked me up, I talked to Jenna. They are going to feature your article on Sunday. And it gets better. It is going to be the featured article in the Life and Health section. Everybody will see it. I can't wait."

"Wow, that's amazing. You're amazing. This is all thanks to you. Let's hope it will get more people coming to the bar. If that place doesn't turn around and start making money, I could be out of a job soon."

"Somehow I have a feeling you'll manage." I smiled and popped a rolled up salami slice in my mouth. Jesse Morrison, super star of Motocross, always had a way of landing on his feet, no matter what challenges life threw at him.

CHAPTER 11

Jesse

Fuck, I hate this stupid phone. Every time I try to get a little shuteye, it rings.

"Yeah!"

"Hey, Jesse. You better get your butt down here to the bar."

"What's up?"

"Some huge, knucklehead dude from New York is here. Says he knows you."

"What's his name?"

"Hold on. Hey bud. What's your name?" I faintly heard a deep voice mumble in the background. "He says…Manny something."

"You're shitting me. What the hell, I owe him a good ass kicking. Be right there. Keep him happy."

A few minutes later I jumped on Kenny's bike and headed for Rookies.

As I entered the bar, a husky voice boomed out, "Jess-eee, my man. Looks like the California climate is working wonders for you…" I was greeted by my two high school friends, Manny and Jeff.

"What the fuck are you guys doing here in LA?" I asked.

"Nice to see you too, Jesse. Way to greet the guy who saved your life."

"What do you mean, saved my life? Last thing I remember was you throwing me out into the gutter, head first. I still owe you for that one."

"If your brain cells weren't fried from all the booze and…whatever, you'd remember that it was *me* who called your brother, Jimmy. Otherwise, you would've been sliced to pieces and fed to their dogs. Ain't that right, Jeff?"

"Yeah, yeah, yeah. What brings you two fuckers to L.A.?"

"I guess you could say we went straight to sin city for some R&R, or whatever. Anyway, we were in Vegas for a couple of days, hooked up with some chick who thought my cock was the proverbial fountain of youth and then I started to get an itchy feeling…"

"Are you sure that itch was from an ethical dilemma or did the *she* turn out to be a dude?"

"Shut up, asshole. I was saying…I decided to take a side trip to the beach. Got tired of that desert sun, and did you know those games in Vegas are rigged? Lost twelve hundred at the stupid craps table."

"Well, you came to the right place. The West Coast girls are tan, tight and fit, although I'm pretty sure they would break under your frame," I teased.

"Fucker. Are you calling me fat?"

"Nooo, I'm just admiring your magnificent physique."

"Yeah, whatever. We can't all be skinny pussies like you." He belted out a hearty laugh. "Man, we sure do miss your raggedy ass in Thunder Ridge."

"How did you know where to find me?"

"Don't you know? You're a fucking celebrity now. There I was in my hotel bathroom, taking a dump, looking through today's paper in search of personal ads, and what do I see? Your ugly face, plastered all over the middle of the page. Talk about a buzz kill."

"Most def," Jeff concurred.

"Damn, they must be desperate for stories here in Los Angeles," Manny continued.

I chuckled and placed my palm on the table. "I fucking love you too, Manny. As a matter of fact, I feel a little bro-mance coming on…"

"No sweat, pal. I figured I'd come look you up and get some free beer."

"The words free and beer never go together when you are involved, Manny. You must be delirious from the road trip, asshole." I laughed and poured them each a Bud. I missed shooting the shit with my New York homies.

Manny and Jeff were the perfect team. Back in New York, Jeff would come over to visit and never ask for anything to eat or drink. Manny would come over and help himself to anything in the fridge, then be the reason I was out of food. Jeff was the friend who would borrow your shit for a few days and then give it back. Manny would lose your shit, and tell you, 'My bad…here's a tissue.'

"Did you hear the news about your mom?" Manny said and drained his glass.

"Haven't heard a fucking thing."

"Jimmy told me just before we left. The doctors are releasing your mom from the care facility next month. She's doing better."

"What the hell? I can't believe that asshole told you before me."

"Well, I was the one who found your mom the night she overdosed on her meds and called Jimmy for help."

"I vaguely remember. I was pretty fucking wasted when you took me home that night."

"Has it ever occurred to you that avoiding alcohol might be a good idea? Saving your ass is taking its toll on me. Ruins my girlish complexion." He mockingly tugged at the outside corners of his eyes with his pinkie fingers.

I snort laughed. Actually, I had curbed my drinking since I met Niki and I was dying to tell Manny and Jeff all about her. I wanted to shout from the rooftop that Niki Milani was my girl, but this wasn't the time. I was so damn excited to have Niki in my life, I would probably gush like a teenage girl; so I cooled my jets and waited for the right time to fit it into the conversation.

"Did the doctor give a specific release date for when my mom can go home?"

"Not exactly, but I think around the time when Jimmy and Sarah are expecting their kid."

"But that's a couple of months away."

"No, it's not. It's next month, September 15th. You're spacing, man."

"Fuck!" Why didn't I know about this? Jimmy must have forgotten, with his mind on the baby coming. Oh well, that might actually work out great. My fingers itched to text my manager and see if he'd booked flights to New York yet.

"Well, the gods must be happy with me today. Actually, Niki and I were planning on going to New York around that time, anyway."

Manny's eyebrows shot up to his hairline and he and Jeff gave each other a look. "Niki? Sounds like you've met one of these hot California girls to call your own," he teased.

"Well, she's something special and I want you to meet her…you and everyone back home. I want to show her where I grew up, where I went to high school, have her meet Jimmy and my mom. You're gonna love her…what?" I stopped talking as I noticed the two of them laughing at me. Then Manny made a gesture in the air like he was cracking a whip and accented it with the sound one makes as it snaps.

"Pussy whipped!" He chortled, his face wrinkled up in laughter and he tipped in Jeff's direction like he was telling him a secret about me, but out loud for everyone to hear.

I scowled. "Bite me." I quickly rubbed the bar top with a rag.

Still snickering, Manny slid off his bar stool and Jeff followed suit. "Well, I'm glad for you, man. Hit me up when you are back in Thunder Ridge. Bring your girl around. I'm sure we'll all scare her off when she meets us. Make sure you bring her to the Oxford Tap, I'm still working there. I'll throw you out again, just for shits and grins…not her, just you." He knocked back the last ounce of his beer and slammed his third empty glass down on the bar top, wiping his mouth with the back of his hand. He turned to Jeff, "You finished?" He nodded. "Let's roll." I came around from behind the bar to say goodbye.

"Jeff and I are heading to the beach to check out some of those skinny bitches you have around here. Wanna come?"

"Nah, I gotta help out here. Catch you later."

"Your loss. Stay safe, bro."

"You too, Manny. And thanks for the heads up about my mom."

We all gave each other hugs, with accompanying manly back slaps, and I walked them to the door of Rookies. As I stood there, watching them walk away, Niki's face appeared in my head. It was unexpected and I focused on it for a while. I thought of her eyes, her smile, her soft voice. What the fuck? I thought of Niki every minute of the day. And for the life of me, I couldn't remember a time when I'd ever felt this way about a girl before. There was something about Niki that made me think of things I normally wouldn't. Things that were authentic and honest. Shit, Manny was right, I've got it bad. I can't believe a guy like me, a roving, injured, motocross rider, with a therapist named Jack Daniels, would even catch her eye for a second, let alone that she would agree to go to New York with me.

I walked back behind the bar and thought of her again, how her long dark hair fell around her bare shoulders when we were alone and she pulls off her top for me. Then when she opens her bra and her tits bounce out…fuck, I just want to put them in my mouth.

Damn, I had to adjust myself again.

CHAPTER 12

Niki

"Hey, hun, are you sure your dad is going to transfer your part of the rent this month? I don't see anything in the account." Kat looked up from her laptop screen with a worried look on her face. Her bare, tan legs dangled from the stool she sat in at the kitchen breakfast bar, wearing shorts and tank top.

"That figures. I knew he would use his money, and my lack of it, to gain control and show that he's in charge. I'll give him a call right now." I was gathering up my large, canvas, tote bag that I used as a book bag and my notebooks to take to class at the Fashion Institute. I retrieved my phone and brought up my dad's cell number from the contact list, but as soon as the call connected it went straight to voice mail.

"Hey Dad. Give me a call back. It's important."

I scowled at my phone before shoving it in my bag. I needed to get to class soon or I would be late again. I had been ditching class and going in late because of spending time with Jesse. I couldn't help myself. He had me wrapped around his little finger. I didn't know if that was a good thing, but I didn't care.

The more I learned about Jesse, the more I wanted to be with him, to spend every second with him. Jesse was the kind of guy who had swag, that spark, that indescribable thing, whatever it's called, that's absolutely perfect. It made him appealing and sexy as hell, just being the person he was put on this Earth to be. He had no question about how he fit into the world; I suppose that's what gave him his incredible confidence. Some people are expert shoppers, and Jesse was good at being his charming self.

I acted like a star-struck teenager around him. Lost all of my rational thoughts. I knew I would have to fight my dad to keep him. But how? My dad seemed to hold all the cards right now: he paid my rent, bought my food, paid for my car *and* car insurance; not to mention he funded my tuition for fashion classes, which he finally conceded to. I didn't know what my dad feared most, losing control or Jesse. All I knew was Jesse made me feel so secure. He made everything seem so clear. I couldn't resist. I just needed to convince my dad of how I felt.

"You know, Niki, if he doesn't pay, I can lend you the money this month, but one month is all I can cover you for. I'm trying to save up money for studio time."

Anxiety twirled in my stomach. I would feel like a real heel if she had to do that. It was Kat's dream to make it as a singer and songwriter. What the hell was

Dad up to now? It wasn't unlike him to pull some crazy shit on me to regain control.

I'd like to think that I had made good decisions in my short life, and this one, choosing Jesse, was one of the good ones, although my dad was chipping away at my self-confidence. That's his strategy and I really hate it; he chips away from underneath until I feel like the whole world will fall out from under my feet and, of course, he'll be the only one there to save me. Well, save me with his money, that is. His moral support hasn't been the type to earn him the 'World's Best Dad' coffee mug for Father's Day.

"I promise I'll get the money, hun. When are you going to record your songs?"

"I saved up two grand but I was told I needed five. It'll pay for five days in the studio. I just hope it will be enough time to record and mix my CD. Pete seems to think so, and wants us to start now. He says he can do it for two grand."

"Who is Pete?"

"Some guy I met after my gig at Key Club. He said he could give me a good deal at West Side Studios."

I turned around from searching the clutter on the coffee table for my favorite note-taking pen. "That sounds almost too good to be true. Are you are sure he wasn't just trying to hit on you?"

"Ha, who knows? He gave me his card." Kat dug in her oversized Coach purse. It was so large it nearly swallowed her head as she poked around inside of it. "I know it's in here somewhere."

It didn't do Kat any good that purses were designed with all those extra pockets on the inside for things such as business cards. Kat always threw anything and everything into the bottomless pit of the largest compartment, like it was some kind of expensive, leather covered, junk drawer.

"Let me look." I grabbed her bag and emptied the contents on the table. "Is this it? Pete Brannon, Music Producer." I handed her a flashy business card.

"Yep, that's him. What do you think?"

"It looks real enough. Give him a call and get it rolling. I promise I'll get the money for the rent from my dad. I just have to do a little more sucking up to him."

"Thank you, hun. Making this CD is one way I can get to the next step in my career. Having a professionally produced showreel will help me get better gigs. Plus, I can sell copies of the CDs after my performance."

"That sounds awesome." I glanced at the clock on the microwave. "Oh shit, I need to be in class... like twenty minutes ago. Let me know when you need me to design some, 'I heart Kat' T-shirts to sell at your gigs." I laughed and twirled my car keys as I headed for the door.

"Absolutely." I left Kat with a huge grin on her face.

~*~*~*~

My phone was on silent but I could still hear the buzzing. "Hello?"

"Niki, there you are. Have you calmed down since our last face to face?"

"Dad, what's going on? Why didn't you transfer the rent money? I thought we had an agreement?"

"What about that boy, Jesse? Is he still around?"

"Da-ad…" I said with exasperation. I heard him snort with a 'humph' in response.

"You know, Niki, I really didn't appreciate the way you behaved at the house at Cinnamon's birthday party. I was very disappointed and you upset Cinnamon. It was her special day and you ruined it with your little tantrum."

"Well, you weren't exactly being very nice to Jesse or me. How could you say those things?"

"Look, a father has to be protective of his daughter against any suitor. It's an unwritten law and you know me, I take the law seriously. Promise me that you'll listen to me. Jesse is trouble. A father can tell. It's not your job to solve everything."

"Well, Dad, you're wrong about him. I'm not fifteen years old anymore. I can decide for myself if a guy is trouble or not. Once you get to know Jesse you'll see that he's a really nice guy."

"I have my doubts. I have some things I would like to discuss with you. Can you meet me for lunch on Thursday? And don't bring that boy of yours. This is between father and daughter."

"Okay, I'll be there, but only if you promise to pay the rent today."

"Alright then, Niki. See you Thursday."

I texted Kat:

"Okay, he's not gonna cut me off...yet," to let her know that my dad would pay the rent today and that she should go ahead and book the recording studio.

I immediately got a reply:

"Already booked! *We start recording Monday. Sooo excited."*

~*~*~*~

"Niki, you're driving," Kat said and threw me her key fob.

"Sure," I replied and cranked the engine. Kat was nervous. It was her first time recording, in a professional studio, with a seasoned music producer. With two thousand dollars of her savings invested, it had better go well.

When we arrived at West Side Studios in Hollywood, we found ourselves in front of a large gray metal gate. I pushed a black intercom button and announced to a squawking voiced fellow that we were here for Studio C. The gate slowly swung open and we parked at the back.

From the outside, the building didn't look like anything special; smooth gray concrete walls and unobtrusive rectangular windows were certainly not very glamorous, considering it was supposed to be a world class recording studio. But as soon as we entered the lobby, the difference was like night and day; we could tell this was a classy place. The décor was all minimalist and sleek, with fluid designs that popped with touches of bright colors throughout the reception area. The floor was polished cement and I couldn't help but admire the wooden 'floating stairs' leading up to who knows where. It all looked very stunning and spacious.

"I can't believe you get to record your first album in a studio like this," I whispered, as we walked in, as if the echo of my voice might disturb the serenity of the room design. I was as excited as a stage mom for Kat at her first professional recording session. I hovered around her, primping her hair, pushing a stray strand into place. She swatted my hand away, nervously scanning the lobby for the reception desk.

"What can I help you girls with?" a young and gorgeously handsome man asked from behind the desk. His smile was so bright he could have lighted the entire northern half of the hemisphere with it. Hollywood was probably the only place where waitresses and desk clerks looked drop dead gorgeous.

Kat squared her shoulders, stepped up and announced, "I'm here to work with Pete Brannon," like she did this every day of her life.

"Who? Pete Branon? Are you sure? We don't have a

Pete Brannon working here." He very authoritatively checked a computer screen behind the counter, as if it might reveal some secret information he didn't already know.

Kat's head swiveled towards mine then back to the cute guy. "Maybe he's just freelancing. He said he works here all the time," Kat said, her voice cracking as her spirit sank.

The cute guy's smile disappeared and it seemed like the lights dimmed. "Sorry, I know everybody who comes here and I've never heard of him. Are you sure it was here at West Side you were supposed to work?"

Kat's shoulders hunched forward and her face was pale as a corpse. I stepped up next to her and interjected, "Kat, give me his business card and I'll give him a call right now."

I entered the number as Kat read it off to me but all I got was a recording saying the number was out of service.

"Bad news, hun. The number's no good." I cringed and wrinkled my nose as I delivered the bad news. "Kat, hun, I think you've been scammed." We turned away from the desk and stepped over near one of the sleek black designer couches in the waiting area. "Good thing you didn't pay him anything yet."

"Fuck! I *did* pay him. He told me the studio needed the money up front in order to get the cheap rate of $2,000 instead of $5,000. Shit!" Kat dropped down on the couch, defeated. "Niki, what the hell am I going to do? It took me six months to save up that money. "

The cute guy from behind the desk came up from behind and addressed Kat. "Sorry about what happened. Are you okay?" He handed Kat a paper cup of water. He seemed genuinely concerned and I was heartened to see that not everyone in Hollywood was an aspiring douchebag.

"It's not the first time I've heard of a scam like that," he said.

Kat looked up at him with embarrassment in her eyes and took the cup. "Thanks. I can't believe I fell for it. I guess when you get desperate enough you tend to believe what you want to hear." She snort laughed. "Sucks to be me."

"No, hun. Don't beat yourself up about it. That son of a bitch needs his ass kicked for taking advantage of you. And our new friend here…" I had to read the desk clerk's name badge, since I didn't know his name. "Our friend… *Elvis*? …here is gonna report that guy for you."

I turned to the desk clerk with a puzzled look. "Elvis? Really?"

He shrugged and laughed. "The guys and I get a little bored here sometimes and make up fake name tags, you know, Elvis, Marilyn Monroe… any name from the stars on the Hollywood sidewalk."

Kat and I looked at each other, tempted to roll our eyes, but at least I saw a little smile peeking from the corner of her mouth.

"Tell you what," he clasped his hands together and rubbed his palms. "Do you have a demo or something?"

"I do, but it's crappy quality. I made it myself. That's why I came here, to record a better demo, an EP."

"If you're talented, the sound quality doesn't matter. Give me a copy and I'll slip it to a couple of people who work here. I'm not promising anything, but you never know. Someone might like it." He gave her a warm, reassuring smile and I threw her a sidelong glance. This guy had better be for real. Kat deserved some good fortune, for at least a little while, after today.

Kat took a recordable CD from her purse. "Thank you so much. You don't know how much this means to me. I'm Kat by the way, *Elvis*." She extended her hand for a shake. "And this is my friend, Niki."

"I'm Conner, that's my real name. I'll see what I can do. Write your name and number on it and I'll call you, let you know if anyone likes it," he said and added a wink to his charming smile. I envisioned him posing for a toothpaste commercial with that magnificent smile, holding up a tube of Crest next to his pearly whites.

Kat scribbled her name and number on the CD and handed it to him.

"Thanks again, Conner." She said as we turned to leave. She picked up her black guitar case and I grabbed her tote bag.

"Thanks, *Elvis*. Hope to see you in a toothpaste

commercial soon." I called back as we started walking away.

"Toothpaste?" he called out. "No, I do underwear commercials," he added with a big smile.

I giggled and pushed the door open for Kat as she toddled through with her guitar case. A couple of minutes later we were sitting in some gnarly, rush hour traffic, heading back towards Santa Monica.

"Kat, I'm so sorry this happened. It really sucks. I know how much you were looking forward to making a good CD."

"That goddamn fucker took my money. What an asshole. Now I have to start all over and find a real producer. How the hell was I supposed to know he was a low life scumbag?" Kat's voice was cranking up in pitch as she reflected on what happened. "I just can't believe I was that stupid."

"You're not stupid, Kat. You were just an easy target for a guy like him. Maybe we will see Pete, the so-called music producer, around one day and you'll get your money back."

"Um, I'm pretty sure there's no way in hell that's gonna happen. But maybe this Conner guy can help. By the way, what was with the toothpaste commercial remark?"

"My bad. Just my screwed up sense of humor." Kat gave me the, 'if looks could kill' stare. "What - the guy had a killer smile. What can I say?" I shrugged my shoulders and pitched one eyebrow up.

"He *was* kind of cute."

"He was damn hot."

"I could see him doing underwear commercials. I bet under that monkey-suit he had a body like Beckham."

"I noticed how he looked at you. I have a feeling he'll be calling you soon, no matter what." I laughed. "So cheer up, girl. Maybe your new friend Conner will hook you up with a legitimate music producer and you'll even get a new underwear model boyfriend to boot."

CHAPTER 13

Jesse

My head was all fucked up now. Pussy will do that to you. Made me all frustrated and irritated whenever I was away from Niki. For the first time in forever, I felt like things weren't impossible, like good luck was right around the corner. I used to want to numb myself when I was in pain; shit, that was just normal for me. I mean, would a surgeon operate without anesthesia? But now I had Niki in my life, I didn't feel the pain. Fucking Manny called it being pussy-whipped. What a joker. Like he would know much about women and love anyway? Oh shit. The 'L' word. Love? *Is that what this is?*

It felt right. Niki was everything I had imagined the perfect girlfriend could be and more. Not that I was the type of guy to sit around dwelling on such matters. I was used to living life on the fly, dealing with shit as it happened and rolling with the punches. I wasn't the type to hold hands and sing 'Kumbaya' while reflecting on the meaning of life.

But Niki…she was beautiful and wise beyond her years. And she had this healing effect on me whenever we were together. Go figure. I didn't know why she made me feel so good inside, but I wasn't going to bust a nut trying to figure it out. I was just stoked that she had agreed to go to New York with me, because I don't think I could last two weeks without her. I'd be a fucking wreck. *And* I couldn't stop thinking about her and how fuckingly, smokingly, gorgeous she was. Yeah! That's what I'm talking about. Bam! Suck on that, *Manny.*

It wouldn't be long until I left for New York for my meetings with team managers and to check up on how my mother was doing.

It had been four days since our bike ride to Malibu and I craved Niki more than ever. After the newspaper article hit, Rookies blew up big time. I was back to a grueling schedule of work and sleep, work and sleep. Every night the bar was packed with people, coming to shake my hand, telling me what a great thing I was doing, helping Kenny with the bar and his bone marrow transplant.

I still felt a little torn about Kenny and all the secrets being spilled. I felt like a punching bag, sometimes. I promised Niki I'd see someone about it; talk out my feelings so I wouldn't be tempted to drink them away. But damn, that shit's expensive. I didn't have medical insurance and I didn't have a daddy who paid for everything. But once I get back into racing, my money situation will be right as rain.

I was damn lucky to finally have a night off. With my fingers curled around my cell phone, I did a backwards dive onto my bed wearing nothing but my birthday suit, since I had just showered. After four days of nothing but freaking work, my mind was flooded with thoughts of being with Niki; being wrapped up in her arms, her soft breasts pressed to my chest. Just thinking about her made me rock hard. She had better be ready to do something to relieve all my tension.

I opened my cell phone to her picture. I added one of her sitting on the motorcycle the day we were up at Malibu. The pic caught the perfect angle of her face in the sun, when the wind blew her long dark hair around her smile. I brought up her number on the screen. She answered right away.

"Jesse, I was just thinking about you," she said. With my back up against the headboard of my bed, I leaned back into the pillows and a slow smile creased my face.

"Who was on top in your little day dream? I want all the juicy details," I chuckled. God, does she know how much fucking self-control this takes? Four days of waiting, four days of desire, just crashed together with all of my raging testosterone and caused my head to feel light and buzzing.

"Ha. Are you picturing me without my clothes on again?" She sounded so delicious over the phone. I wished she could have felt what I was feeling. Every flash of exquisite, mind numbing pleasure she brought me.

"Oh baby, you have no idea." What this girl did to me rocked my world, and everyone else's within a hundred mile radius, just with the sound of her sweet voice. "I'm off work tonight and there's nothing more I'd rather do than come over, have you wrap your legs around me and rock you for the rest of the night." I thought I heard her breath catch. "So, what are you thinking?"

"Well, I am sitting here in a very thin T-shirt and no bra and oh it's soo cold in here I think my nipples just poked through my shirt."

She was so devious. I think I fucking growled or some shit like that. "Listen, my agent wants to book the tickets for us to fly to New York. He needs some personal information about you for the airlines. So how about I come over and we can get that squared away?"

"You better come over tonight or I'll have to spank your sorry ass."

"You are a bad, bad liar. Don't go making promises you can't keep," I snickered. "I'll be there at seven. Do you want me to bring some food?"

"Sure, how about Chinese? I'll teach you how to use chopsticks like a pro."

"Perfect. See you at seven."

CHAPTER 14

Jesse

The hours of the afternoon passed quickly and before I knew it my shift was over and I was free to go see Niki. I passed a tray of used beer glasses over the bar top to Chase, when a familiar voice popped in my ear.

"Wow. I can't believe how you guys have turned this place around."

"Kenny! Geez, you scared me there." Kenny had to shout to be heard over the pop music playing in the bar and it caught me off guard. Customers were talking and watching the latest sports games on the various TVs mounted on the walls. I whirled around and gave Kenny a big smile. He looked better, healthier.

"It's packed. This is great, Jesse. Business hasn't been this good for months." Kenny was beaming. He leaned in slightly, like he wanted to tell me a secret. "I hope I can keep up tonight." He was pumped to be back in his bar and running the show. It was written all over his face. Chase gave him a nod and a hello from behind the bar.

"You look good. How do you feel?" Chase called out over the countertop of the bar.

"Not bad. The two day break from the chemo helps immensely. That shit sucks the energy right out of me."

We pressed through the crowd and worked our way to the open aisle at the end of the bar, and went around behind it, to the cash register area. Watching him jump right in and work the register made me realize how important his job was to him. I looked at him differently now, with the knowing that we shared something. We both loved our careers and we'd had them taken away from us, at least temporarily. My injuries were healed and as soon as Kenny finished his chemotherapy I would be able to give him my bone marrow and he'd be fully recovered in no time.

Life was looking good and in two short weeks I'd be in New York, visiting my mom, wondering how or if I would even approach her with my new knowledge. I didn't want to tell her the truth about Kenny while she was still in the care facility. Who knew how she would handle it. Shit, I wasn't sure if I wanted her to ever know the truth. Maybe it would be better to just let sleeping dogs lie and besides, I had more pressing things on my mind right now.

"Glad you could fill in for me. I got a little hurricane named Niki waiting on me and it's been four days without…" I wiggled my eyebrows up and down. "If you know what I mean."

"Yeah, whatever. You go have fun. Even though I may look like a corpse lately, I'm not dead yet, you know." Kenny laughed. He worked quickly, expertly prepping the mixed drink station for Chase.

"You don't get to use that against me. Well, Kenny, I hope you can survive tonight. I don't think Chase can handle all these customers by himself. I don't want him to call and interrupt me." I patted his back.

"You better get your ass out of here before I change my mind."

"I love you man, I really do but… I'm out of here." I spun on my heels and headed to the door. "And no monkey-business from the two of you." I wiggled my index finger back and forth from Chase to Kenny, feigning a stern face. Kenny chucked a nasty, dirty bar towel at me, but I ducked, laughing, and it missed me.

Ten minutes later I was inside Chung's Chinese takeout, ordering practically half their damn menu. I had no fucking idea what Niki liked so I got a little of everything.

"You have big party tonight?" the guy behind the counter asked with a huge, toothy smile. Apparently I was his biggest customer of the evening.

"Throw in a couple extra of those fortune cookies while you're at it. I need some good fortune tonight."

"You got it, mister. Have good night. See you soon." He bowed and handed me three bags of food. I tipped him an extra ten bucks. His smile grew even wider, as if he couldn't express his gratitude in any other way.

I sprinted up the stairs to Niki's apartment and rapped a beat on the door.

A voice called out through the thickness of the door, "Coming." Two seconds later I was feasting my eyes on Niki. She was freaking gorgeous, in a short tight fitting dress, her long dark curls falling down around her shoulders just the way I picture her when I wake up with a hard on and…oh shit, there it goes again. "Wow, you look hot," I said as I dropped the bags on the floor and grabbed my girl. "And you smell fucking amazing too." I sniffed at the sweet scent coming from her neck.

"What took you so long?" She rose up on her tiptoes and threw her arms around my neck as I brushed my lips along hers, all the way to her lips. I pulled her into my chest. It felt good and warm with her there, up against me. "I've been excited all afternoon…"

I silenced her lips with mine and ran my hands through all that loose hair, imagining how I could mess it up even more with her naked in bed. I pulled away and exhaled. I had my fix, at least enough to tide me over until later, when I planned to fuck her six ways to Sunday. "Sorry baby, I had to show Kenny a few changes we made at the bar to more easily accommodate the rush of customers coming in, as a result of *your* brilliant idea. So technically, it's your fault I'm late," I said with a smile.

"Excuses, excuses." She gave me a coy look. She pushed a stray lock of hair behind her ear. "Tell Kenny

I'm just glad I could help," she continued and bent down to pick up the bags of food. Her arms stuffed with the three large paper bags from Chung's, she headed to the kitchen. "Are we expecting company? These bags are huge." She laughed.

"I wasn't sure what you liked so I got a little of everything." I snatched two of the bags to lighten her load and carried them to the table where she had already placed plates, napkins and even a couple of burning candles. The apartment looked warm and cozy. The candlelight flickered and reflected off the wall, making everything in the room appear warm and fuzzy. I stood behind Niki and circled my arms around her waist as she worked on taking the food out of the first bag and placing it on the table.

She leaned her head slightly to the side, giving me personal grazing rights to the side of her neck as she worked.

"You are so amazing," I murmured against her neck. "This looks great with the candles, Niki. I've been waiting for days to get you in my arms like this, four tortuous, lust filled days…"

"Did you bring any wine?" She paused, holding a container of fried rice poised for its landing spot on the table amongst the other Chinese dishes.

I jerked my head up "Fuck, I knew I forgot something. I can go get some."

"It's okay." She set the box down. "I think there is a bottle in the fridge." She peeled away, out of my arms, to retrieve the wine. She looked almost fairy like, walking barefoot to the fridge, her hair swooshing out as she spun free of me.

I looked down at her feet with a puzzled expression. "Where are your shoes?"

She giggled and returned with the uncorked bottle in hand. "I'm a free spirit. I can wear what I want in my own apartment." She pushed down on my shoulders. "Sit down, sweetie." She poured me a glass of wine, smiling an endearing - yet wicked - smile. The shoes didn't matter. She wanted me. That's what mattered. As incomprehensible as that was to me, at times, I was just damn pleased as fucking punch that this gorgeous, smart, and talented girl wanted me. What made her want me? Hell if I knew. I wasn't a lawyer like her last boyfriend or even the kind of guy who traveled in her dad's circle of friends. They were all refined and educated. And I was…not.

After what seemed like an hour, we sat with dirtied plates shoved aside. The red candle wax had melted down the sides of the two glass holders. Niki leaned her elbows on the table and swirled pale gold Chardonnay, watching as it rotated in the glass. She looked up and I couldn't even speak. I didn't want to speak, I just wanted to enjoy the view. We sat that way for the longest time, savoring the moment. I held her stare, smothering myself with the look in her hooded green eyes. Finally, Niki interrupted the silence. "Let's take our wine to the living room and relax on the couch."

She stood and came to my side, trailed her fingertips down my arm, leaving a rash of goose bumps in their wake, and gently pulled me behind her by the wrist. After lowering the lights, she gracefully carried the two candles into the living room and placed them on the wooden coffee table with our wine glasses. I slouched back into the soft cushions of the couch and gently patted the seat next to me, a signal that I wanted her perky ass next to mine, right under my arm, which was draped across the back of the couch. But she'd have none of that, just yet. So I watched, studied her, adored her for a few moments, with the candlelight casting elegant shadows on her beautiful face.

"You said your manager needed my information for the plane ticket to New York."

"Yes, just your full name as it appears on your ID and birthday."

She reached for a pen and notepad from an end table, which was of the same matching design as the wooden coffee table, and scratched something on the small white paper. She handed me the note and slipped into the space I had carved out for her under my arm. "I wrote it down for you. Here…"

March 17 1991. Note to self: Remember that date for future reference.

"Thanks, he will order the tickets tomorrow, I think." I smiled and pocketed the note. She reached for her glass of wine and tucked herself up next to me. I pulled her close, burying my nose in the gentle waves of her hair and inhaling its scent.

"I'm glad you arranged your class schedule so you can come with me."

She tipped her head up and gave me a warm look. "I can't wait to go to New York."

"How do you feel about meeting the rest of my crazy family? You know Kenny and the story of my screwed up family tree…"

She rested the back of her head against my arm and looked up to the ceiling as she spoke softly. "Mostly excited. I'm glad your mom is better but I'm a bit nervous about meeting her."

"Don't be. She'll love you, baby," I said and took her hand. My eyes followed the slope of her nose, tracing her profile in the dim light of the room. I had never seen anyone as beautiful as Niki looked tonight, settled here next to me on the couch. Not just because she was gorgeous. Because she had agreed to go with me to New York and meet my family. She didn't even know how much I wanted her there. How much I needed her support. Even if it was only for two weeks.

"Has anyone told your mom about Kenny being your dad yet?"

"Jimmy knows; but we agreed it's better to wait, so I can tell her in person. After we meet with my team managers in Manhattan, we'll head up to Thunder Ridge. I'm sure it will be a shock for her. I just hope she takes it well."

Niki smiled encouragingly. "Let's hope so, anyway.

Keep a positive attitude. Women are mysterious creatures. Haven't you heard of women's intuition? She may have suspected all along. Women can sometimes tell these things, you know."

"Tell me about it." I sure as hell couldn't figure out women. If I could, I'd write a book about it and make millions of dollars. Who was I to say why my mom did what she did? I was sure she had her reasons and maybe I was about to discover them. Or maybe not. Shit. Maybe I didn't want to know anymore. Ignorance is bliss; maybe I should just let it be and let everyone move on with their lives.

"She never acted like she had any suspicions. Plus, that year Kenny lived with us after my dad died, she didn't really act like she wanted Kenny around. You know, if she'd wanted a relationship with Kenny, that would have been her opportunity. But then Kenny left." I glanced down and realized that my hand was clenched tightly against my thigh. *Relax, idiot. Don't ruin this time with Niki.*

"How do you feel about Kenny now? Have you come to terms with any of this?"

The conversation just took a turn down the deeply personal isle. I inhaled.

"It's hard to forgive someone after a betrayal. I thought I knew him. Hell, I was living under his roof, eating his food, helping at the bar, yadda, yadda…you know the story. And then bam, the shit hit the fan and I'm in a world of hurt. So I thought about it all and hey…we're family. I mean, so Kenny tarnished my view of him – get over it. My dad died when I was a kid – deal with it. Family members lie to each other all the time. So what? Forget about it and move on. I was tired of all the pain and hurt so in my mind. I forgave him."

She stared at me again, her eyes seemed full of admiration and awe. "Jesse, that's so great. If you were seeing a therapist they would be doing the happy dance. It takes some people years to get to the point where they can forgive."

"Now I just have one more hurdle with my mom, when we get to Thunder Ridge. I have to take it easy on her. She'll just be getting out of the care facility. That's why I need you there with me. You're my mainstay. You will keep me from going high and to the right."

"I'm excited to meet her and I'll be there for you, whatever happens, babe," she murmured and placed her slender hand on my arm. I fought the urge to lay her back on the couch and kiss her until I couldn't breathe. But she smiled at me and everything felt right in the world, which was unusual for a sorry ass bastard like me. So I settled for cuddle and talk time.

"I love this time of year in California, when the really hot heat of the summer is over."

"You're going to love upstate New York in September. Be sure to pack clothes for cool weather, especially for night…and the leaves on the trees…the colors are *fantastic* at this time of year…" I stopped talking and watched her face, monitoring her for signs of recognition.

I noticed that Niki became distant. Her gaze flickered and it seemed like she was on another planet all of a sudden. She blinked and looked up at me, coming back to life. I waited a few seconds before I cut through the silence.

"Hey, are you okay, Niki?" I took her wine glass out of her hand and set it on the coffee table.

"Sorry, I just spaced out there for a moment." She sat up on the edge of the couch with me and pushed a strand of hair behind her ear.

"I noticed. You were like in a different world. What were you thinking about?"

"I was thinking about our trip and...sometimes I zone out like that. It's something I have been doing ever since I was a kid. I have ADD, you know."

"Oh, is that a problem for you? You don't seem hyper at all, to me." She relaxed and leaned back into the couch again and pushed her hair up with one hand, holding it momentarily then letting it fall. I wished she wouldn't do that because it just tempted me to grab her. I cocked my head to the side and studied the delicate, beautiful girl on the couch beside me.

"No, I don't have the hyper element but I sometimes have trouble focusing on tasks or conversations."

"Oh, I see. Do you take anything, like medication, for it?"

"Not anymore. I used to, as a kid, but it messes with my ability to be creative. That's not so good when I want to be a designer, I kinda need to be creative to do that. So I avoid the drugs and that's why I zone out from time to time, like you just saw."

My heart warmed as I stared at this incredibly perceptive woman. She had more shit to deal with at school than I had realized. It must have been a challenge to study with ADD and she had already completed one degree. She was even more remarkable than I had thought.

"Niki, you amaze me every day, the more I learn about you. I can't wait to show you off to my family. But did you hear me tell you to pack some warm clothes?" I felt like an idiot; I didn't know if when she 'zoned out' she remembered what we were talking about or not. "And the part about the leaves?"

She laughed and swatted at my arm. "Geez, Jesse, I'm not deaf… Of course I know about the weather and the trees and the leaves in New York. I lived there, remember? I told you I went to boarding school there for a while."

"Sorry, I'm a duffus. You did tell me but I'm afraid I'm remiss in my duties as a good boyfriend and I haven't been hanging on your every word…so refresh my memory, please." I gave her my best puppy dog eyes, which drew a smile from her.

"Okay, pour me some more wine. It only seems fair. I know your crazy life story, now I'll tell you some of mine."

I obliged and settled in, stuffing a small decorative

pillow behind me, as I reclined.

"After my mom died, I kind of didn't take it very well." She changed her position and pulled her legs up, so she was sitting cross-legged on the seat of the sofa. "I had trouble in school. I didn't even want to go to school, so I ditched. And at home, well, I became a royal little bitch. I missed my mom so much, Jesse. It just hurt so badly and all I wanted was for her to come back. So I screamed, threw tantrums like a two year old, anything to stop the hurt… and so on. That's when my dad couldn't handle it anymore. But you already know this part." She shifted on the couch, holding the wine glass in one hand and tracing around the rim with the finger tip of her other.

"Yeah. You told me this much the night we went to hear Kat perform. What happened after that?"

She closed her eyes and then opened them and paused for a moment while she stared into the wine.

"Do you know what a 'cutter' is?"

"Yeah, go to any school and ask, 'Do you know anyone who cuts?' And everybody knows someone. But you, Niki? That seems so unreal that you...oh baby, I'm sorry." A pain stabbed my heart and a fierce urge to protect her flooded my body.

"Yes, that was me, back in sixth grade."

"Sixth grade? That seems so young. I thought it was more high school age kids who did that."

"Not any more, now younger kids try it. And I was no different. It eased the emotional pain I felt after her death."

"Did your dad know? I mean, at first?"

"No, it's easy to hide under long sleeves, but when he finally found out he freaked! He sent me to a therapist, but that didn't help much. I basically refused to cooperate and started acting out in school. After I had been suspended for the second time in a month, for smoking weed, he decided that sending me away to boarding school was the only solution. He said it was to help me get better, to help me get over Mom's death. The therapist said kids like me, who are very sensitive, use cutting because of what's going on in their family life. As strange as it may sound, it's a way of getting control of your life. And go figure it, there I was, living with my control-freak of a dad."

"Well, he is *that* for sure. Wasn't there anyone else you could have gone to, like to an aunt or uncle?"

"Not really. I was just a regular kid with a shitty dad and a repressive home environment. Don't talk about your feelings, don't discuss it, just sweep them under the rug, and whatever you do, don't show any sadness. What a bunch of bullshit. I was a kid without a mother, for Christ's sake. It was his fault and I still believe he did it just to get me out of his life. He was weak and spineless. He couldn't deal with a kid with deep emotional problems. And he was afraid it would look bad for his law firm, which was ridiculous. Half his clients are drug users anyway; not much difference, if you ask me."

A sour, mocking tone trembled in her voice. She gripped her wine glass tighter with both hands. I was stunned at what Niki had to endure, the pain of losing her mom and the rejection from her dad. *God, what an asshole!*

"That is so fucked up. I'm so sorry you had to go through that, baby."

Her eyes looked wet as she continued her story, and my pulse picked up. I wanted to reach out a hand, but I was riveted to my seat. "Did the boarding school help?"

"Oh, holy hell, no. The boarding school was horrible. It was a bunch of emotionally fucked up teens, all cooped up in the same place, and almost every week there were incidents or episodes; you know, drugs, out of control behavior...I couldn't handle it."

"Jesus, Niki, that sounds horrible. How was that place supposed to help anyone?"

"And then, one night, I cut deeper and harder. I woke my roommate with my screams. The counselors told my dad and he thought I was trying to commit suicide, that I cut more that time just to get attention. But the thing is, you feel better when you cut. There's a kind of weird painkiller effect that you get. When you are in emotional pain, you literally don't feel that physical pain as much when you cut yourself."

I nodded, almost in disbelief of what I was hearing. How could I even pretend to fathom the level of pain she was revealing?

"Wait, Niki. If you were at this place to get help,

away from your dad, what made you want to cut deeper like that? Why didn't you stop hurting yourself altogether?"

"There was this guy. An older student." She let out a long exhale. "He was…the typical rich boy, with a dad who was a senator, or something like that, I don't remember exactly. But his shit didn't stink and no one could touch him with a ten foot pole. All the girls liked him and I was pretty young and impressionable; I was in about the seventh grade, so I was excited that he liked me. It made me feel special that he was attracted to me, when he could have had his pick of all the girls there."

Oh God no, if this is going where I think it is… I couldn't believe the torrent of words flowing out of her mouth, it made my skin crawl. My jaw twitched. I wanted to say so much to her about how I felt, let her know she could tell me anything, that there was so much more to our relationship: friendship. But I remained silent. She wasn't finished. She had just spilled a shit load of emotional baggage and I'd be a damn fool to cut her off now. I could see in her eyes that she wanted to tell me this. She *needed* to tell me and get it out, so the hurt wouldn't come out in other ways, other self-destructive ways.

I glanced at Niki, but she didn't look back at me. She looked up to the ceiling and pursed her lips then continued. "Well, one day after the dinner meal in the dining hall, we snuck out to this little grotto-like area on the school grounds, with lots of trees and bushes. Kind of a park-like area. He had some weed and we were gonna smoke it and get high. We started kissing and stuff, then he got more aggressive, started pushing for more. His hands were all over me and he shoved his hand down my pants really roughly, saying, 'Come on, come on you'll like it. If you don't do it, I'll make you do it.' I wasn't ready for sex yet and even if I had been, I certainly didn't want it that way, forced on me...anyway, the more I resisted the more he fought..."

"God, Niki, how did you get out of there?"

"I kicked him in the balls really hard and ran like hell. But not until he had left a few bruises on me. Then that was the night I cut myself again and the counselors and everyone thought I was relapsing, thought I was suicidal."

"Didn't you tell them what he did to you?"

"Hell yeah. But they didn't believe me; he was the senator's son, the golden boy. You know, like Jason is my dad's golden boy. I hate people like that. I hated him and I hated my dad for believing someone else and not me, his own flesh and blood. I hated Jason for being the 'golden boy,' for wallowing in his privileged status, for sucking it in and using it to his advantage over me, like a pig rolling blissfully in putrid muck." She paused for a second, almost gasping for air.

"Hey, I get it, baby."

"Sorry, I went off on a tangent there, but the point is,

if a person feels like they can't say no, or stand up to people, they end up believing they are not allowed to do that. Especially girls, especially *me,* after living with a control freak. I felt like I had no voice, no one believed me, like I was just some worthless piece of shit that God had crapped out. Who would ever like me? Hell I didn't even like myself; no wonder my dad sent me away. And if you can't control someone else's behavior, then you control your own so… I cut."

She uncrossed her legs and leaned back into the couch, her body language saying, 'There you have it. Now you know why I'm all fucked up.' I felt like I had been hit on the head with a goddamn board. It all made sense now. Her freaking out, back when I got in a fight to save Chase; it was a reaction to her childhood trauma. My heart hurt for her. It felt like someone had taken a huge, rusty, railroad stake and pounded it into my heart with a sledge hammer. I felt so incredibly bad for her. I wanted to rush out and find that asshole, and all the counselors, and pound their fucking faces into the pavement for what they did to her. And Jason – I knew I should have kicked that sorry motherfucker's ass, the night I met him, at Cinnamon's birthday party.

"I've never told anyone this before, except the therapists of course. I have a hard time trusting people, but I want to trust. I want to love…"

Niki was trembling and when she tipped her head back and closed her eyes, big wet tears rolled down her cheeks. I slid in closer to her on the couch and wrapped my arms around her, pulling her head into my T-shirted chest and hugged her. "You're safe now. You can trust me, Niki. I'm here for you and I always will be."

For a long time I just held her tightly, nuzzled against my chest. A few more silent tears rolled and I pushed her hair back from her face and lifted her chin. I got lost in her gaze and I kissed her soft, moist lips so she knew that I meant what I said, so she'd feel it in her soul. I meant it. Her pain was my pain and I wouldn't let her feel alone ever again. I'd eat bullets for her like a champ, be her warrior. No one's going to mess with my girl again.

Fucking ever!

She breathed in deeply and let the air rush out from between her lips. I brushed away her tears with my thumb. I kissed each spot on her face that had been wet, as if the mere action of a kiss could erase all the toxic memories that spewed forth in her tears. Like cauterizing a wound, sealed with a kiss. She held my gaze and blinked. Could it work? Was it possible? Could the love invoked through a kiss really heal?

As if she had read my mind, she softly said, "You don't know me. My relationships with men usually turn to shit and my dad has been wreaking havoc with my life for years."

Slowly, I reached out and ran my fingers through her long dark hair and all the way down her arm to squeeze her hand. "Call me crazy, but I feel I've known you my entire life and don't worry about your dad. I keep my promises."

"But what about your career, Motocross? How can we be together if you travel the world half the year and I'm here?"

I lowered my face close to hers, my breath on her parted lips. I felt the warmth of her body close to mine. I inhaled her. My pulse quickened and I whispered, "Don't worry, baby. I don't have the answers now, but we will figure it out. We have all the time in the world." I wanted to take her into the bedroom and lay her out on the bed and show her with my entire body how much I cared for her, but that would look like I was being too forward. After all, she had just spilled her guts to me about her past insecurities, leaving her feeling vulnerable. Divulging the secret of your defenses to the offense leaves a person wide open for the other to know their weaknesses and allows the possibility of being taken advantage of. That was the last thing I wanted to do to Niki. I wanted to protect her, not take advantage of her.

I watched the expression on her face as I cradled her in my arm and stroked the smooth skin of her cheek. Slowly, she closed her eyes then opened them and looked up into mine. In a soft voice she said, "Baby, let's go into the bedroom."

"Are you sure? It's okay if you don't want to..."

She placed her hand on my face and nodded, "I do. I want to lie with you and feel you all around me, your arms your legs, all of you."

I stood up, trailing my hand down her arm to her hand, and pulled her up off the couch to follow me, but as soon as she was upright she hung her arms around my neck and wrapped both of her legs around my waist. With my hands supporting her sweet ass, I held her up and kissed her, feeling her push hard against my mouth, with fervent passion.

I walked her to the bedroom and gently placed her onto the bed. I softly and slowly seduced all the clothes off of her. I gently kissed every inch of her naked body and not until she pleaded my name did I enter her. We made love, panting and writhing, twisting our bodies together into the wee hours of the morning. It wasn't until all the bed covers had been ripped off and flung onto the floor in gnarly balls that she fell asleep in my arms. She looked so peaceful and content. I had never been this happy in my entire life.

CHAPTER 15

Niki

It was official. The Roxy was the hottest nightclub in Hollywood. Call me opinionated, but I loved this place. The music was loud and the drinks were strong. Jesse and I were meeting Kat and Chase for some SoCal craziness and maybe a little dancing. The Roxy also lent itself to a parade of sexy stilettos, which I refused to forgo, even for the comfort of dancing. Kat would unequivocally agree. No chick was drool worthy if they weren't wearing the shortest skirt with the hottest heels. Although I had Jesse, I wanted every guy in the place to be envious of him as we strutted through the door, because Jesse was the baddest bad boy, in charge of my heart, and I wanted him to be proud of me. It didn't take long to spot Kat and Chase in the sea of partygoers. As usual, Kat was expertly working the crowd at Roxy's in her spiky heels.

"Ni-i-ki-i!" Kat came toddling over, waving her arm in the air; her yellow purse, which matched her skimpy yellow dress, reluctantly dangled from her elbow as she walked. "Fuck, you won't believe it. That Pete guy who scammed me out of my money is here." Kat tipped forward to give hugs all round, holding her drink out as she leaned in.

"You're shitting me. Where?"

"See that guy, standing over there next to those two girls? He's wearing a sports jacket with a black shirt and dress pants. That's him."

"Are you sure?"

"One hundred percent. *That's* the cock sucker." She stabbed an accusing finger in the air as her petite face screwed up into a hostile glare.

Chase came up from behind and greeted us, giving me a hug and Jesse the guy slap. "Kat filled me in about the scam that dude pulled on her. She wanted to go kick him in the balls, but I convinced her to wait until you got here, Jesse. Did Kat tell you about it?"

"Yeah, that shit is cold. I think we need to go fuck him up. I'm just saying." Jesse shrugged and raised an eyebrow.

"Let's go have a little chat with him," Chase said.

"Wait!" I said, "Let me handle that scumbag."

"No way, Niki. Chase and I can take care of this. Don't get me wrong, but this is not the kind of thing for a woman to handle. He'll eat you up, spit you out and pick his teeth with your fingernails."

"Okay, that's a gross visual, but whatever... Look Jesse, I can do it. I have an idea."

"Alright, but I'm not letting you go up to him alone. I'll be right at your elbow if anything goes down…" He jerked his head at Chase. "Come on, buddy."

Kat trailed along behind.

Adrenaline pumped through my veins like a locomotive. I wasn't so much scared; just angry at this guy for tricking Kat and stealing her money. "Don't say anything. Just let me do all the talking." I spun to my right and searched for Kat's large suitcase of a purse. "Kat, do you still have his business card?"

"Yep, it's in here somewhere." She pawed in her purse, but her organizational skills were hopeless.

I sighed. "It's okay. I'll think of something to say."

"No, I got it right here." She pulled out the card in triumph.

"What'd you do? Clean your purse?"

She gave me a smug smile and handed me the card. *Pete Brannon, Music Producer. Yeah, more like Pete Brannon, fuck stick scam artist.*

We pressed our way through the throngs of party people in the engorged club. As I walked up to Pete, Jesse followed right behind me. The guy was leaning against the bar checking out two girls, grinding on each other in tight, short, club attire, on the dance floor.

"Pete, right? I said and he turned to face me.

He looked at me confused. "Sorry, do I know you?"

"Not really, but my friend told me you are a music producer."

He looked at me suspiciously. "Sorry, you got the

wrong guy. My name is Michael." He turned his back on me and leaned on the bar.

"Oh really? So this isn't your card?"

His head swiveled and he flashed a look of disdain over his right shoulder at the card I held up in the air between my index and middle finger. In a dismissive gesture, he returned to nursing his drink, then spoke to the air straight ahead, and arrogantly sipped his scotch on the rocks. His voice was cold when he answered. "Never seen it before."

Jesse and Chase had walked up behind Pete and heard everything. Jesse grabbed Pete's arm.

"We'll see about that," Jesse said and picked Pete's wallet from his rear pants pocket. His black dress slacks made it slide out quite easily.

"What the fuck are you doing? That's my wallet! You son of a bitch!" He wrenched his arm free and the two stood face to face.

"Who the hell are you?" he demanded.

"I'm the asshole telling you to watch your language in front of the ladies."

Jesse flipped open the leather wallet and immediately located a couple of glossy business cards, identical to the one Kat had been given. "What do we have here, my friend?"

"I'm not your friend." he grumbled.

"So you've never seen that card before…Michael?"

Jesse twisted the open wallet around and cocked his head to read the driver's license through the clear plastic pocket inside.

"Wow, your name really is Michael. The police will be interested to hear what our friend here has to say about you." He nodded in Kat's direction. She stood behind us, like a dog straining on its chain.

"Yeah, you mother fucker! You took my money you shithead! Fuck you and fuck your…" She rose up on her toes and spat the words as I held her back. With Jesse around, fists could start flying at any moment. But, this time, I wasn't worried about it. Sure, I was trembling. My pulse was racing, but this time the rush felt exhilarating.

Jesse's face was contorted with anger, his nostrils flared with fury and his face was a red mask of rage. Veins bulged, blue, on his neck, as if the fire in his blood threatened to burst right out through his skin. He pitched his torso forward, to get in the guy's face, and Jesse's dark look was so sharp it clawed at the guy like talons.

"She will be happy to report how you *scammed* her for two grand. You're in some serious shit, motherfucker! Is that what you call producing music? Scamming people? You're nothing but a low life scumbag."

Jesse pulled back and tossed the wallet with all the other contents intact at the guy. The man flinched and reeled back as the wallet bounced up against his chest and he caught it. Jesse threw a fast sidelong glance at Chase, whose muscles were tight as a rope, ready to strike if needed. Jesse wasn't taking his eyes off this guy for a minute. The tension in the air was so thick you could cut it with a knife.

"Niki, call the cops." Chase ordered.

"How about we kick his ass first and then call the cops," Jesse shot back.

The guy's face paled with fear. "No, no! NO! Please, no need to call the police. Look, I don't have it. I gave it to my dealer. I…I…I don't think he'll give it back."

"Tell him you want it. Tell him you want a Dancing Elmo for Christmas. I. Don't. Care. Just get the money!" The pitch and volume of his voice propelled his words like a cannon, attracting curious stares from people standing nearby.

The guy looked nervous but stalled, like he was plotting his escape, about to bolt for the door. With a strong, angry fist, Jesse twisted up the guy's suit jacket by the lapel and pulled him in within inches of his face. He seethed at the guy with mounting rage and spoke through clenched teeth.

"See this. This is my happy face. Either tell me where her money is or become an invalid, bitch." He threw the words at him like stones.

"Okay, okay. I got your friend's money. It's at my house."

"Now we're talking. Let's go get it."

"Look, you two wait for me here and I'll go get it."

"Excuse me. What are you on? Because you must be hallucinating. There is no sign on my back that says

Jerk Face." Jesse's clawed hand clamped down on Michael's shoulder. "We are coming with you to pick up the money. Niki, you stay here with Kat. Chase and I will go."

"Jesse..." I held onto Kat's arm and stepped out of the way. "Be careful." I had no doubt that Jesse could handle himself with this guy. I had seen him easily beat the living daylights out of that guy who threw a beer glass in Chase's face. His ability to unleash a torrent of violence was dependent on his pent up anger, his unresolved emotions. It was strange how unfettered rage could be an advantage. I shuddered inwardly as I thought of various scenarios. This guy could be armed, have a knife or worse, but my fears were pacified with the realization that Jesse had always held his own in the past and that Chase would be with him.

A minute later, Jesse and Chase left, with the scumbag wedged between them, as they hustled him out the door. Kat and I parked ourselves at a small corner table until they returned. I swallowed another drink in the hope that it would wash away the anxiety of waiting.

Kat worked her lower lip between her teeth, fiercely punching the keypad on her phone. I wasn't sure why she bothered. Neither Chase nor Jesse would answer a text, given the situation at hand. She looked up. Her trepidation was obvious in her eyes. "I hope everything goes well. I would never forgive myself if something happened to Jesse and Chase over a stupid two thousand dollars," Kat said.

"Everything will be fine, and two thousand dollars is not stupid." Even I was stunned when my voice came out even and calm. Maybe my self-confidence really *was* growing. I was standing up to people and the shaky, uneasy feeling in the pit of my stomach had dissipated. Tonight I had confronted a bad guy with nerves of steel! Well, maybe more like nerves that were not wet noodles. Let's not get carried away here. *Baby steps, baby steps*.

Four empty drinks glasses later, there was still no sign of Jesse and Chase. A tiny bud of nervousness threatened to spring up inside me, but I sheared it down, like a weed in a garden. I could try calling – but it was highly unlikely he'd answer.

"Fuck, where are they?" This time Kat was nervous and I the stoic one.

"Hold your horses, girlie. Let them work their magic."

Finally, I spotted Jesse coming through the door. He ran his hand through his unruly hair. My heart did a little flip as he strode towards our table. The sight of him always quickened my pulse. He and Chase forcefully pushed through the crowd, looking like two Viking warriors returning from battle. I could finally breathe again.

Their faces were unreadable, not offering a clue to how things had gone. Assuming the worst, I blurted out, "You didn't get the money?"

Chase plopped down in the chair next to Kat and Jesse slipped in next to me.

"What happened? What happened?" Kat squeaked, her energy was so pent up she could barely keep her petite tushie on the seat of the chair.

"The fucker ran away." Chase blew out a breath.

"Shit! Now we will never find him." Kat's misery was so acute her physical pain came through in the tremor of her voice.

Chase threw his head back laughing and nearly rocked the chair to its back legs. I didn't see what was so funny. These two just went away with a crook, an underhanded thief, probably with gang affiliations. My imagination exaggerated the situation but his laughter didn't make sense.

I turned to Chase and asked, "Do I get an invitation?"

"To what?" He chortled, barely able to contain his laughter long enough to speak, as he rocked back and forth as if he were riding some kind of damn rocking horse.

"To whatever festivities are going on in your head, obviously. What the hell, Chase?" I looked at Jesse for an explanation. He ducked his head and put a hand on his brow, resting his elbow on the table. He faked rubbing his forehead in an attempt to shield his smirking face from my sight. His efforts were in vain. The jig was up.

Even Kat was grinning from ear to ear, caught up in

the infectious humor found only in Chase's mind. "Damn, Chase. What's so funny?" Kat asked.

"You should have seen Jesse…" He had to pause to suck in air. "I've never seen anyone run that fast. In thirty seconds flat he chased down the dude." Chase rocked back again and slapped his thighs. "It was fucking awesome."

"I hope you kicked his ass, Jesse," I said boldly.

"Wow, listen to you, babe. I can't believe you just said that. What happened to always finding a peaceful solution?"

"Yea, well, maybe I changed my mind. There's a time and a place for everything. Besides, that bastard deserved it for what he did to Kat. Men like him think women are easy targets. But we are not. We can show the world that no one can take advantage of us and get away with it…well, maybe with a little assistance from some men, guys like you. Men who use their powers to fight evil…"

"I'm no Spiderman, Niki. Wait…" Jesse's face went deadpan and he reached over one shoulder and patted around on his back with the palm of his hand on his T-shirt. "What's this? I think I feel a cape or something on my back…is it red?"

"Yeah, yeah, yeah, I get it. So Spidey…did you get Kat's money back?"

Jesse reached into his back pocket and pulled out a thick white business envelope. "Here you go, Kat. It's all here."

Kat's eyes went wide as saucers, and her mouth opened with a gasp.

"Jesse, you *are* a fucking hero." She launched herself straight up and over the small cocktail table, knocking empty glasses as she dove. She threw her arms around his neck and planted a big juicy kiss on his cheek. I grabbed the edge of the table to steady it as it wobbled. Then she launched an attack on Chase next, profusely thanking him and all of us again and again for helping her retrieve the money. Luckily, he was positioned next to her and the contents of the table were safe from her enthusiasm. She seemed to linger a little longer with her arms draped around Chase's neck and his kiss was a little more lingering when she thanked him. My eyebrow shot up. Was it my imagination? Or did I see a sign?

"Come on, guys. Let's get out of here," Jesse said and shoved back his chair. "What do you say we stop by Rookies for a nightcap?"

Ending the evening at Rookies, with Jesse and my two best friends, sounded like the perfect way to celebrate. I gave myself a pat on the back. I had made progress today. I was learning to live in the moment, go for the gusto, and ohmygod, 'seize the day,' - carpe diem. I stifled a giggle.

Jesse had shown me how to let go of the worry, all of the 'what if' thoughts that were so confining. There had been times in the past when I had drummed up so many 'what if's in my head that I'd been immobilized.

Left unable to think straight or move forward. But, tonight, I had made a breakthrough. Sure, I wasn't all the way there yet; I still had that little voice of doubt, that whiny little voice buzzing like a fly, but I had definitely improved.

Jesse threw his arm over my shoulder and we all headed out the door of The Roxy. I gazed up at him, with a huge smile plastered on my face. He beamed down at me and gave me a warm kiss on the forehead, as our feet hit the sidewalk of Sunset Blvd. in West Hollywood.

CHAPTER 16

Niki

"Are you nervous about flying?" Jesse asked as we stepped up to the check-in counter at LAX airport. Here I was, inadvertently heading back to New York State, a place I vowed I'd never return to, after my years spent there in boarding school. It was with mixed feelings that I stood next to Jesse and my brimming suitcase, waiting for it to be my turn to show proper identification. Although my memories were sullied with negative thoughts, I reminded myself over and over, in my head, that this trip had a positive purpose. This time, New York would get a second chance to show its colors, no pun intended. Hopefully the dark memories would be replaced with more cheery ones. The kind that would later be nostalgically pressed into a drug store photo album, or nowadays, ostentatiously posted on Facebook to share with all my family and friends.

"No, not at all. I've flown many times, my dear."

"Some people still get nervous when flying, even if they've done it often."

"Are *you* nervous?" I asked. I found it peculiar that Jesse, a man with steel nerves, who took the hairpin curves of Motocross tracks like they were a walk in the park, would have *any* fears, let alone a fear of *flying*.

"Hah, no way. I like flying. Actually, it reminds me of a flight I took about a year ago to Paris. I met…a-ah, never mind." He stared off into the air as if his mind had warped back to a time of pleasant memories.

"No, tell me. I want to know."

"It was just a fun flight, that's all." He ducked his head and reached down to grab the handle of his suitcase. He heaved my bag, and then his, onto the stainless steel shelf where the attendant had politely instructed him to put them.

"Hmm, really? That's all? You are not going to tell me what was so *fun* about it?" I peered into his twinkling eyes. The corners of his mouth twitched, struggling to keep a humorous smile at bay that threatened to erupt. *That devil.* Only a fond memory could provoke such a cryptic smile.

Two unruly locks of hair fell loose into his eyes when he leaned over to pick up the bags. He shoved them back with his hand. "Uh, just a lot of bumps and stuff, you know…turbulence."

My heart skipped a beat without warning, it did that more and more ever since Jesse entered my life. Yes, I had 'Jesse Syndrome;' it strikes women out of nowhere. First, you experience shortness of breath and difficulty breathing, then a rapid rise in heartbeat. This is followed by complications of 'fuzzy thinking,' whenever Jesse's enigmatic personality is near, and thoughts get confused. It often leads to impulsive behavior that one wouldn't normally engage in. And I had my suspicions that it struck women from New York to L.A., and even possibly as far afield as Paris.

For a brief moment I imagined that all the women in the airport terminal were gawking at him, drooling over his good looks and the rippling muscles that stretched his T-shirt to its limit. I snapped my head around for a look, then chided myself for acting so ridiculously. What exactly was he talking about? He looked like a boy caught with his hand in the cookie jar.

"Hmm, so turbulence is fun now," I muttered. Half of me wanted to believe it was nothing, but the expression on his face made me wonder. I was sure there was more to the story than he was telling, but I decided to let this one slide and brushed it off. We all have at least one innocent little secret and I decided to let this skeleton stay in the closet.

The clerk behind the counter handed us our boarding passes and, after the usual security check including a full body x-ray scan, we were sitting comfortably in the Business Class Lounge, waiting for the flight to start boarding.

"That's a nice benefit of business class. Access to

the airport lounge," Jesse said, practically stuffing an entire cream cheese breakfast Danish into his mouth at once.

"I've never flown business class before. Nice change, so far."

"Really? Your dad never splurged on you when you went back for Christmas breaks and such?"

"He was always tight with money on certain things. He has an anal retentive driven logic about money. I could never figure it out. If it pleased him to spend money on something, then he'd splurge and go all out. If he perceived it as too expensive, then he didn't. Like I said, there seemed to be no logic to it, more like it was controlled by his anxieties about money."

"Yeah, I guess if I had to pay out of my own pocket, I would fly monkey class too. Thank God for team managers and their big budgets," Jesse laughed as they finally called out on the loudspeakers for the boarding of our flight to JFK, New York.

After an uneventful flight, with no major turbulence, we walked towards the baggage area to meet up with the driver. I noticed a sharply dressed man holding a sign saying, 'Morrison.' Cool, that was us.

"Hi, I'm Morrison," Jesse said to the driver.

"Welcome to New York, sir. Are those all of your bags?" He looked at our two pieces of luggage and started loading his trolley.

"That's it."

Soon we were riding in the back of a black, stretch

limo toward the Midtown Hilton Hotel in Manhattan. That would be the first leg of the trip before heading upstate to Jesse's hometown of Thunder Ridge.

I was out of my mind excited to see Manhattan. Despite my many years attending a New York State boarding school, I had never actually been to The Big Apple. Home of the headquarters of Vera Wang. She was, in my eyes, a fashion design god, or goddess in this case; I worshiped the fabric laden ground of the Garment District that she walked on. I had been to the Garment District in L.A. and my feet were itching to hit the pavement of the one in Manhattan, to see how they compared.

Never in my wildest dreams had I ever thought that I would one day study fashion design, base the focus of my design style on Vera Wang, and be in the very part of the very *city* where her headquarters were located. What were the freaking odds of that happening? It was just too much of a coincidence, in my book. And it was all thanks to Jesse. It was almost like the universe had opened up and tapped me on the head with a fairy wand.

Tap. Tap. Pay attention, Niki.

I had just reached for another sip of my white wine when a waiter, in a black coat and crisp white shirt, delivered our meal to the elegant table, which was draped with white linen. My first day in Manhattan with Jesse had been amazing and this restaurant, with its cozy atmosphere and the chargrilled smell of meat in the air, was the epitome of a New York City steakhouse.

"What time is your meeting tomorrow?" I asked, over mouthwatering plates of the city's finest cuisine. This was one of Jesse's favorite places and I could see why he, and everyone else, had fallen in love with this cosmopolitan wonder.

Manhattan was so different from Los Angeles. It was like someone had sped up the camera of life. Everything and everyone crushed together, shoulder to shoulder, at a faster pace than I was accustomed to. I saw throngs of men and women, all dressed in suits, actually walking on the sidewalks, unlike in L.A., where everybody huddled in their cars, suffering in bumper to bumper traffic jams.

Of course, nothing beat the shopping in Manhattan. A girl could go broke very quickly here, buying shoes alone. Kat was going to love me. She had told me, in no uncertain terms, when we first moved in together that all of my shoes were to be considered 'community property.' It was her good luck that we shared the same shoe size. I had a feeling the pair of Dolce & Gabbana heels I just purchased, from the shoe gods of the same name, would be her favorite pair to borrow when I got back.

Throwing me a sexy smile, Jesse drew down his beer

and cut into his thick Delmonico steak. "I have to get up early. My first meeting is with Laurent, my agent, at ten a.m. Then I have two meetings with team managers in the afternoon. You can sleep in, if you like. Laurent and I'll meet up with you for lunch. You'll like him. He's very energetic and funny. He has the craziest accent, though. He's originally from Switzerland and he's a smooth talker. He'll talk your ear off, so…you've been warned." Jesse stabbed a chunk of steak with his fork and waved it in the air before popping it in his mouth.

A different side of Jesse appeared before my eyes. I had never regarded him in the light of being a professional at anything, other than charming my wet panties off of me. He seemed to be taking on the aura of a true expert in his sport. He wasn't just all about dirt and well…bikes. I liked it.

"Laurent always closes the deal and that's what really matters. If it wasn't for him, I doubt I'd be where I am today. Getting on the right team means everything, in this sport, and he delivers."

"He sounds like an amazing guy. I'm excited to meet him." I tipped my head to the side and peered up to the ceiling. "You know, Jesse, life is funny sometimes. How we find ourselves bumping up against the most special people, the ones who can change your life. Isn't that really what it's all about? If you want to be successful in business, sports, or even just in life in general, it's all about the relationships, creating great relationships and finding those perfect partners. Let's toast to relationships, of every kind, and the success of your career."

"Hell, yeah!" Jesse said with a grin that stretched from ear to ear.

I lifted my wine to his beer and the rims of our two glasses touched, releasing a joyful clink of glass on glass, sealing the toast with an audible agreement.

Chapter 17

Niki

I was minutes away from the restaurant, on my way to meet Jesse and Laurent, contending with two shopping bags full of fabulous designer clothes slung over each arm, when I heard the familiar ding of my phone. I juggled my load, and expertly whipped my phone out of my purse. Although my arms were heavily laden with bags, I could find my cell phone with my eyes closed, if needed. I was like a soldier who is trained to assemble his gun, piece by piece, while blindfolded and hanging upside down with a bomb about to explode. I didn't need to stop walking or even look at my purse. My fingers were calibrated to its touch.

It was a text from Jesse, *"We're running ten minutes late. Get us a table. It's reserved under Laurent's name, Garcon."*

I walked into the restaurant. It was a tapas place,

decorated Spanish style.

"I have reservation, a table for three. Name is Garcon," I said to the host.

"Oh yes, Ms. Garcon. Your table is ready. Right this way."

"My name is no—," I attempted a response, but the host was already too far ahead of me to hear.

He pulled out a chair. "Here you are. Your waiter will be right with you. Would you like for me to store your bags while you dine, Miss?"

"No, that's fine. I'll just put them here." There was enough space for the bags between my chair and the wall. I wasn't going to let them out of sight and maybe forget them. I texted Jesse that I was already seated at the table.

"Almost there!" he replied. His excitement was contagious. I could feel it through the phone. Jesse was really in his element now, gearing up for a racing tour around Europe, hopefully with a new team. Despite all the excitement, a nasty question nagged in my subconscious, a thought I had been forcing to the nether regions, not wanting to think about it and give credence to it. What about me? What about us? Hopefully, the tour wouldn't affect what we were building. Anyway, I didn't want such thoughts to sour my experience here in New York. I'd cross that bridge when I came to it.

A couple of minutes later the two of them arrived, Jesse striding into the room with fearless confidence, overshadowing his agent, and everyone else in the room for that matter. I stood up to greet them. Jesse leaned over and gave me a kiss, running his hand down my back and pressing me into his lips ever so slightly. Laurent greeted me with a huge white smile that contrasted with his sun kissed skin. He looked to be in his forties, bald but sporty, and tanned.

"So, this is the beautiful girlfriend you've been bragging about, Jesse. You certainly weren't exaggerating. You look stunning, darling," Laurent said with a delightful accent.

Jesse ducked his head and smiled. "Niki, meet Laurent, my agent."

"It is absolutely my pleasure," Laurent said kissing both my cheeks, European style.

"Likewise," I replied. This guy really was a smooth talking Johnny, just like Jesse described. "I have heard a lot about you."

"All good things, I hope." He winked at Jesse and we all sat down.

The food was amazing as was the company. Laurent was indeed hilarious. I could see why he was such a great agent. He was one of those people blessed with a knack for talking and entertaining, that ability to make witty conversation roll off his tongue with perfect timing to punctuate the humor. I imagined that if Laurent weren't an agent, he would make a great stand-up comedian.

The last of the ice in my glass had melted into water and it was time for Jesse and Laurent to go to their first meeting of the afternoon. They had to leave post haste.

"See you later, at the hotel, baby," Jesse murmured in my ear as we waited for their cab. Laurent was busy studying the screen of his cell phone and Jesse took a moment to slip his arms around my waist, from behind, for a stolen moment of affection. He squeezed me in his strong arms, his muscles flexing. His warm breath puffed on my ear and sent little shiver up my spine.

"As soon as I'm done with these meetings I'll be back to our room. I hope to find you stretched out on the bed in something black, lacy and sexy." I closed my eyes and a smile slowly curled my lips. As I basked in the visual, the cab door flew open and Jesse peeled himself off of me to jump in the back seat with Laurent.

I walked back to the hotel to drop off my morning purchases and slip into some good walking shoes for round two. I felt exhausted. Shopping, walking and processing all the new impressions had almost worn me out. But I wanted to make the most of my first time visiting Manhattan, where the famous Garment District was located. It was one of the most notable fashion capitals; design trends created here were mirrored around the world. I took a deep breath and waited for my second wind to kick in as I headed to the elevator.

Once outside, I headed mid-west in direction, toward the Garment District. I was in awe. To think my feet were touching the same ground as the valiant women's garment workers from 1911, to Calvin Kline, Ralph Lauren and the likes, modern designers whose very

182

names oozed fashion. I explored shops loaded with endless bolts of fabrics, colors, and textures, milled in Italy, Switzerland and France. The sensitive nerve endings on my fingertips registered information that my eyes could not as I gently rubbed each piece between my thumb and forefinger. Some shops had reasonable prices that fit even the average person's budget.

The place was over the top. Creative possibilities popped into my imagination like fireworks on the Fourth of July, each one producing another, "Ooo, look at that one," or "Aaah, look at *that* one." My mind whirled with ideas for flowing dresses and trendy tops. The possibilities were endless. I could buy several yards for my next project at school and really wow my teachers at FIDM.

While scouting out the best fabrics in the world, it really dawned upon me that fashion design was absolutely what I was meant to do. My dreams were solidified. The last remnants of doubt in the back of my mind had vanished. I belonged here, among all these fabrics. Diverting my plans from being a lawyer to fashion design was not the mistake that my dad made it seem. It clearly was what I wanted to do with my life. The desire to take this magnificent fabric and create amazing dresses from it was like a raging river, being held back by a faulty dam. I don't think I could have kept it contained if I tried. Now that I had taken a few design classes and got a taste of what it felt like to let my creativity flow, the dam was about to burst. To hell with my dad and his control issues. How dare he make me doubt myself? It was my life and I would damn well do with it as I pleased. There are only a few events in a lifetime which clearly show the path one is meant to take. This was undoubtedly one of them.

CHAPTER 18

Niki

It was getting late and, with bags full of fabric, I hailed a cab back to the hotel. When I returned to the room, Jesse was already there, his damp hair looking like he had recently showered and changed clothes.

"Hey, baby. You are back already? I thought you had another meeting?" I asked.

He came forward and kissed me, reaching for my bags and unloading my sore arms. Fabric can be heavy, even when there's only a few yards of it.

Testing the weight of the bags he asked, "Damn, what'd you buy, bricks?"

I chuckled, "No silly, just the most awesome, fantastic fabric for my next project. Jesse, you wouldn't believe this place. The Garment District here beats the one in L.A., hands down. But I'll show you later. So what's up with your last meeting?"

"We cancelled the second meeting." He looked at me with a serious expression.

"Why? What happened? Is everything okay?" He put the bags in the closet and walked back to face me. I met him halfway. He slipped his arms around my waist and I inhaled his fresh soapy scent. I touched his strong jaw with my fingertip and traced down its edge. I searched his blue eyes for the answer. He was playing with me. I saw it there in his eyes. And then he burst.

"Everything is freaking fantastic." His mouth widened into a big grin. "Yamaha wants me back on their team as their lead racer. They're sending the contract proposal next week."

He picked me up and spun me in a circle that ended with him plopping me on my back, bouncing on the bed. I squealed a laugh as the momentum of his playful gesture caught me off guard.

"That's amazing! Congratulations, baby. I'm so happy for you." I said breathlessly, the mattress still giving up one last bounce.

"You know, we should celebrate. Normally I would take you out to the most expensive restaurant but really…all I want is to order everything on the room service menu and spend the night here, in bed with you. What do you say?"

"That sounds like the best idea you've had all week. I'm too exhausted to go out anyway." I lay with Jesse's firm body pressed above mine on the bed. My hair had fallen back when he flung me on the bed and my neck was exposed. He nudged my chin with his nose and I rolled my head to the side, an open invitation for his lips. With me pinned underneath him, he feathered soft kisses up my neck to my ear, gently pulling my earlobe into his mouth and sucking. A hot tingle raced through my body and I gave a pleasurable sound of confirmation.

His voice was low and alluring when he murmured in my ear, "Why don't you take a shower while I order and meet me back on the bed wearing something sexy that I can pull off with my teeth." His last words were punctuated with a firm thrust of his pelvis.

I imagined feeling his skin against mine, feeling his mouth on mine. I needed to taste him. I buried my fingers in his thick hair and, with both hands, pulled his mouth to mine and kissed him hard. His tongue darted in my mouth, and swirled around mine. I wanted him now; right here, right now. The ache in my throbbing loins demanded immediate attention. I didn't know if I could wait until after dinner. Jesse pulled back from the kiss, leaving me breathless, mouth open and wanting more.

He gazed into my eyes, two stray strands of hair hanging down, and spoke softly and tenderly. "You are amazing, Niki. I'm so happy you came with me. I always want to be with you."

I reached up and pushed back one of the dangling strands of hair, cupping his face in one hand. "Me too, baby. Me too." That's where I wanted to be too, always in his arms. I closed my eyes, feeling a buildup of happy tears behind my eyelids that threatened to slide down my face.

In one swift move, Jesse pulled me tight to his body and flipped both of us over so I was on top. He smacked my butt with a firm wallop, using the palm of his open hand. A sharp crack split the air and I yelped, letting out a sound like someone had stepped on a little Chihuahua dog.

"Get in there and take your shower, girl." I rolled off him and jumped to my feet, holding my behind with my hand, like a child that had just been spanked. He popped up into an upright position, sitting on the edge of the bed and said, "I want to eat dinner soon. I can't wait for dessert and you're the specialty dessert on the menu tonight, baby."

"You guys and your one track minds…" I teased as I ducked into the bathroom for the fastest shower of my life. I couldn't wait either and wanted him desperately. I was excited to try out something very special from my Victoria's Secret collection that Kat had convinced me to purchase just for this trip. Something that would make his eyeballs roll up in his head just looking at me.

As soon as I emerged from the bathroom, my wardrobe choice jerked Jesse's attention my way. I teased him with the typical movie pose in the bathroom doorway, dressed in a matching red lace set. Red for the hot passion I felt coursing through my veins as I studied his frame - broad, young and strong.

Neither of us could eat much. We were too interested in moving on to the 'dessert menu.'

"Now this is the way to have dinner," Jesse said when we were finished, running a finger along the lace edge of my bra. The sensation of his finger brushing against the crest of my beast rekindled the before dinner thoughts and within seconds my pulse was racing again. Jesse pushed the room service cart to the side of the bed and slipped the do not disturb sign on the outside door handle. I took that as my cue to slide up on the billowing white comforter on the bed and seductively pose with my back to the headboard, high heels and all. I reached to remove the shoes.

"No." Jesse stopped me with his intense gaze. "Leave them on. You look damn hot all up on that bed. And I have a little dessert for you."

"Mmmm. Mr. Morrison." I bent one knee up and pushed my hair up onto the top of my head striking a kind of 'pin up girl' pose. I wanted Jesse begging for more. "Come here and show me what you've got, baby."

Jesse's voice rumbled deep in his throat. He stepped over to the dinner cart and pulled a sweating bottle of champagne from a bucket of ice. He strategically set two empty champagne flutes on the linen covered cart and popped the cork with a bang. I flinched and giggled.

"What's the champagne for?"

"Technically, it's not champagne, it's Prosecco -

sparkling wine - but we're celebrating my deal and me getting back into racing. Plus, my mom is getting better and Jimmy's about to become a proud papa and….well the list goes on."

He neatly filled the glasses with Prosecco, then reached for the silver plate cover on the same cart and lifted the lid. He dramatically held the lid in the air and said, "Something sweet for my sweetie." The raised lid revealed a small white porcelain bowl, filled with shiny red strawberry halves, glistening in the reflection of the lights in the room.

Jesse dimmed the lights and two seconds later, strawberries bobbed buoyantly in the effervescent bubbles, as Jesse dropped a couple in each glass.

"And I want to celebrate you?"

I looked up sheepishly from under my lashes, sitting with my back against the headboard and holding my glass with both hands. He raised his glass.

"To one of the most special and exciting things in my life right now…you, baby."

I smiled, feeling foolish for being so egocentric and wanting all of his attention. But I did want it. I wanted to drink in every ounce he had to offer. I wanted to feel like I was the only woman in the world for him, the center of his universe, the only person who could make him feel special. It was an unflattering assessment to be so greedy. I wanted him all for myself, but at least I considered my thoughts to be legitimate for in the bedroom.

He sat down on the edge of bed, facing me, with his thoughtful eyes on me, caressing my body with his warm gaze. He lowered his voice to a sexy hum and said, "I am so glad I met you and this feels like a dream to me, that a girl like you would want to be with a sorry ass guy like me."

The delicate glass rims of our stemmed glasses kissed with a clink and we sipped the wine, eyes locked on each other, almost daring each other to be the first to break away. Reaching out his arm, he set his drink on the small food cart adjacent to the bed.

I watched the muscles ripple under the taught skin covering his bicep as his arm moved. I loved watching his body, especially his eyes when he made love to me. He slid his warm hand up my leg, snaking around to the inside of my thigh as he moved forward and rose up between my legs to reach my lips for a kiss. A shiver of desire ran one second ahead of his hand, running up my body as the heat from his hand caressed my skin. Only his touch made me feel like this, made me want to beg for more. His lips were still moist from the champagne and he tasted sweet. The touch of his lips was a delicious sensation, as his tongue traced the edges of my mouth. A new spiral of ecstasy shot through me.

His lips left mine to nibble my neck. "I'm glad we ordered room service and stayed in," he murmured.

Between kisses he took the glass out of my hand and placed it on the bedside table, then brought his attention back to me. I pushed my hands through his long locks of hair, those glorious locks that fell in his blue eyes; those sexy locks and those sexy eyes. I pulled him in and his lips recaptured mine, more demanding this time, making me desperate to feel his tongue grazing mine.

His lips slowly descended feathering kisses down my neck, all the way to the swell of my breasts, pushed out high and round by my bra. His lips grazed the area, fingers pulling at the lace edges, eager to sample my nipples, already sensitive and swollen, under the fabric.

I gently pushed him off and sat up, with the intention of removing the object of his frustration, but decided to opt for a little teasing fun first. I reached for a strawberry and wedged it between my breasts. With a challenging look in my eyes I said, "With a cherry on top…or in this case, a strawberry."

"Mmmm, I like. Told you, you were my dessert tonight," he grinned and leaned in to my chest, taking the fruit out with his teeth while he reached behind my back and unfastened the clasp of my bra. My breasts bounced free and he tossed the red temptation aside. When sexy lingerie doesn't stay on long, it's a sure sign that it was worth the expensive price tag.

He sucked the red berry into his mouth and held it there until his hands were free. He pushed the strawberry out of his mouth far enough to grasp it with his thumb and forefinger, then he took a bite, to release the juices, and slowly rubbed the remaining piece on my nipples, first one and then the other. A cool sensation shocked my skin and the stimulation of my hardened peaks shot a tingling line of fire all the way down between my legs.

"That's cold…" I giggled, and watched him lick the sweetness, as he took each nipple into his mouth one at a time. After his last lick, he brought his head up to my line of vision, smiling a devilish grin. His smile melted into a lusty gaze as it blazed straight into me. I couldn't tear my eyes away from the steamy stare of those half-hooded blue orbs. I thought I heard a kind of deep rumbling moan that was part chuckle, erupt from his throat. Whatever it was, it jolted my heart and made my pulse pound faster.

I wanted him badly and I wanted him now. I wanted him to crush my lips with his and possess me. I wanted to touch and kiss every square inch of his skin, every part of his hard body, especially the part that was getting harder by the minute. I wanted to ride the crashing wave of an orgasm with him inside me, but I could tell from the look in those bad boy eyes that he was going to make me beg for it. He was going to torture me with a slow tease, and make me ache with the desire of a slow burn, before giving me what I wanted.

My eyes follow his motions as he gently touched the small sweet piece of the strawberry to my lips. Reflexively, I parted my lips, eyes still locked, and he slowly rubbed the fruit across my lower lip, then slipped it into my mouth, along with his finger. Looking up at him, I clasped his hand with both of mine, holding his finger in my mouth. I closed my warm wet lips around it and slowly sucked, gently thrusting it in and out, in and out. His hardness jerked in spasms between our bodies and a hurricane began to rumble inside of me.

By now he was between my legs, on his knees in front of me with his finger in my mouth and a sky high erection. I leaned forward and replaced his finger with his erection. He moaned, sucking in a sharp breath through clenched teeth, arching back with a jerk. I moved my mouth around his velvety smooth shaft, letting the sensation fill him, reveling in the satisfaction that I was pleasing him. My blood surged in a lusty frenzy inside my veins. I moved faster, increasing the rhythm. I felt his hand swirling in my hair, guiding me, and I imagined him savoring the sight as he looked down at my head moving on his cock.

He gently put his hands on my shoulders and pulled out of my mouth, laying me back on the bed. He scooted back and caught me behind my bent knees, and pulled me down the bed until I was flat on my back. I gasped at the urgency in his sudden, commanding move. I liked it. It fueled the hot desire already searing through my veins.

He reached for the champagne glass and took a sip. I lay there, panting, barely able to keep from clawing at him and pulling him on top of me. He gave a seductively wicked low laugh as he fished a strawberry out of the happy bubbles. He slid his hand up the inside of my thigh and tugged the red lace panties off with one hand. He pushed at the inside of my leg and I eagerly opened my legs for him, aching for his touch to take me to that special place. The firmness of his warm palm felt good as he caressed the thick part of my thigh, the erogenous part on the inside, where the skin is smooth and nerve endings tantalized and tingled. He squeezed, and rocketing sensations fill my brain with anticipation. Pleading words burst from my lips in the form of his name, "Jesse…"

He pushed his hand up further and slipped his fingers into my folds. I bucked and thrust my hips in the air, imploring him to touch me where I needed. I was swollen and the concentration of blood in my hot spot, caused my nub to throb with an intensity I had never felt before. My skin was so hot I feared I might internally combust if he didn't give me relief soon.

I arched my back and flung my head back, biting my lip to keep from whimpering out loud. With his fingers still holding the champagne infused strawberry, Jesse parted my folds with his free hand and put the cool wetness of it on my fiery bud. I gasped and contracted. Intense pleasure waves spiked through my body as he rubbed the fruit along the outer edges of the lips of my sex. He traced a path up and around in one direction, then up and around in the other, licking the sweet trail behind it with his tongue as he worked the strawberry over the surface of my pink skin.

The little piece of berry was getting pretty mashed

up by now and in one final swirl his fingertips pushed it right on the button. He sucked hard, drawing it and my clit into his mouth. He flicked and swirled with his tongue. I wrenched and moaned, hitching my breath with deep sounds of raging pleasure. His tongue moved frantically; it was all wetness down there. The perfectly slippery prologue to what I needed next, to feel him inside of me.

He held my hips down and worked faster, he was going to make me come in his face, before I could get him to penetrate me. I felt it coming; the waves of pleasure came now in torrents. He wound me up and my body begged for release. My muscles tightened, my fists twisted knots in the bedspread cover as I panted and rolled my head from side to side, begging for more.

My awareness of reality was slipping away. The rush was so fantastic, so extreme, I thought my body would explode. I squealed a high pitched sound.

Oh my fucking God!

And screamed out my orgasm into the New York night.

With my mind reeling and my brain flooded with endorphins I was barely aware of him on top of me. I clawed at his shoulders; I pulled and tugged, desperate to feel his skin on my skin, his chest pressing into me. He was like an animal, wild and virile, holding his cock at the base and throwing his head back. He drove it in me, hard, not holding anything back. I surrendered, I pushed up to meet his every thrust as he pounded and stroked the living daylights out of me.

I pulled my legs up and wrapped them around his waist. He convulsed and contracted on top of me, his face buried in my neck, my long hair splayed all over the pillow. A deep groan rumbled from his throat as he shuddered into me. With my arms around his neck and my legs around his waist, I clung to him, our two bodies creating a symphony of love.

CHAPTER 19

Jesse

A rush of satisfaction that stemmed from returning home after being away hit me, hard, as we drove into the city limits of Thunder Ridge. I was stoked to be back in this little shit-hole of a town. The sight of familiar shops was like a soothing balm for my soul, as we made our way through town towards my brother Jimmy's house. I had only been gone a little more than three months, but my drunken escapades in this town, and repeatedly getting thrown out of the Oxford Tap by Manny, all seemed a lifetime ago.

And who would have thought I'd met the most wonderful woman while on a crazy adventure in California. It was only supposed to be a visit, to help Kenny with that damn bar of his, but…who would have thought?

I glanced over at Niki, at her radiant face. She

looked like a freaking angel. Her long dark hair fell in large curls over her shoulders. She turned toward me and gave me a smile. It was as if the sun had come out for the first time that day. She was perfect. I was falling for her hard, and I savored it. In the past I would have gotten drunk and hit the road, or messed it up long before anything serious could develop. Not this time. No fucking way. I was in this for the long haul. Press it to the limits and see where we would end up. I trusted her more than anyone. *Maybe this was what love was all about?*

We hadn't made a commitment yet, or actually said the words. Although I had been tempted many times, I was still a little gun-shy. It would feel awesome to hear her say those three little words to me. But there was still so much I didn't know about her. And, of course, there was her disapproving dad. Fuck him! I was sick and tired of other people trying to meddle with our relationship. This was something only Niki and I could touch.

As we drove into the driveway of my brother's small house, Niki was fidgeting with her hands in her lap.

"Nervous, baby?"

"A little." Niki dug in her purse and whipped out some kind of lip gloss stuff. She flipped down the mirror on the back of the sun visor. She didn't need it. Her lips were just fine for me the way they were and if she didn't stop massaging them with that applicator thing and opening her mouth in the perfect shape for…oh shit, we'd better get inside quick.

"Everything is cool," I said. "Jimmy and Sarah don't bite." I gave her a quick kiss of approval and tore myself away. I climbed out of the rental car and stretched my legs.

"You smell that, Niki?"

The woodsy aroma of autumn leaves filled my nostrils as I inhaled. "That's the smell of home." California had its own unique smell of the ocean, but nothing beat the crisp scent of Thunder Ridge in the fall. I peered through the window at Niki, still sitting in the car.

"You okay?"

She looked at me and smiled. "Perfectly okay. I'm just excited."

I opened her door and she stepped out.

"Cute house," Niki said.

"It's pretty small. Most houses here are. You'll like the town, friendly people, nice people…well, most of them," I chuckled. "Except for Manny and Jeff. They're a little on the crude side."

I reached out my hand to knock, when the brown door flew open and Jimmy's grinning face appeared. "There he is. My little shithead of a brother."

"Right back at you, bro."

"Glad you made it. What took so long? It's only a seventy five mile drive. I was beginning to think I needed a magazine…" I gave him a big bear hug.

"Jimmy, this is Niki."

His eyes flicked to her and he raised a brow. "Very nice, Jesse." Then he addressed Niki and said, "A very lovely lady. You come with high praises and I can see you live up to all of them and more. I'm Jesse's big brother, the asshole cop."

"I kind of figured," Niki said with a smile. "I mean the part about being his brother...not the other. So excited to finally meet you. Jesse's told me all about you."

"Oh, I bet he has, a pile of crap I'm sure. Come on in. Say hi to my wife, Sarah. She's in the family room taking a load off."

We walked into the house and I almost choked when I saw Sarah in a slightly reclined position, small green couch pillows supporting her back. *Holy shit, her stomach is huge.* "Wow, I didn't know you were carrying triplets. Jesus, how can you even get up off the couch and do housework like that?"

"For Christ sake, Jesse, show some fucking sensitivity, you heathen," Jimmy said. Niki scowled at me and gave me the 'shut up, dumbass,' swat on my arm.

Sarah looked me up and down then shook her head. "Yeah, yeah, you're real funny, Jesse. A regular comedian. Do I look like I'm laughing? You fucking try carrying this load, twenty-four seven. You wouldn't last five minutes, you wimp."

Sarah was busting my chops. Normally she was the petite flower type, but her condition had her acting like a little firecracker today and who could blame her with a…shit, a damn watermelon in her stomach. Or maybe two watermelons.

"Sorry, I'm an idiot. When are you going to pop?"

"Not soon enough." She shifted her pillows. "My due date is Friday. Sit down, sit down, you two." She waved to an overstuffed burgundy loveseat that matched the couch. "Jesse, you dickhead, where are your manners? Introduce your girlfriend."

"I'm Niki. Nice to meet you, Sarah. You do look uncomfortable, it must be so tough." Niki took a seat next to me on the loveseat.

Unable to find a satisfactory position, Sarah moved her body again and let out a sigh. "If I'd known I would have a kid this big, I would've fucking adopted. Imagine trying to pop this thing out of your vagina?"

"Um, I don't have a vagina, Sarah. At least the last time I looked," I said.

"Yeah, well half the time you act like a pussy…" Jimmy shot back.

"What the hell was I thinking?" Sarah fussed again with the small green pillow supporting her back. "You did this to me, Jimmy, you fucking did this and you're gonna pay." Exasperated, she yanked the pillow out and tossed it at Jimmy with a jesting smirk.

Jimmy moved to her side, handing her the pillow and asked, "Can I get you anything, baby? Anything to make you a little more comfortable?" She shook her head and flipped her middle finger at Jimmy, giving him a suffering look. "The doctor says it will be at least ten pounds," Jimmy said.

Niki turned to me, wide eyed, and mouthed the word, "WOW."

Jimmy patted his wife's knee. "Jesse, why don't you show Niki your room and unload your bags. I want to take you for a little drive later."

"Sure thing, bro."

I slung our two suitcases into the tiny guest room. Sarah had already painted the walls a pale blue. I maneuvered our bags around an unassembled baby crib that leaned against the wall and flopped Niki's suitcase onto the bed.

Niki spotted a lamp on the dresser, a recent purchase, no doubt for the baby's room. She walked over to it and leaned in, touching the base of the lamp.

"Aw-w-w. This lamp is adorable. Look Jesse, there's a little bear holding balloons. I have to get a baby gift. Maybe a cuddly teddy bear, like this one, to go with the theme of the room."

"You'll just find any excuse to shop, won't you?" I teased and unzipped the suitcase on the bed. She gave a sidelong glance like I had given her a challenge. Her expression softened.

"I really like your brother and Sarah. She doesn't take shit from anybody, does she?"

I shook my head and grinned. "They're awesome together. You wouldn't think it, when you see them, but they love each other." I handed her a clothes hanger from the closet for her dress.

"Oh, I see it. Jimmy seems so gentle and sweet."

"Yeah, try growing up with him for a brother."

"Oh you don't mean that. He admires you. Anyone can see that. Besides, it must have been tough for him, being the man of the house at such a young age."

I stole a few moments alone with Niki to pull her into my arms. I pushed her long dark hair out of her face and leaned my forehead against hers. "I suppose you're right." I cupped her face in my hands and tasted her sweet lips.

I was interrupted by the sound of Jimmy loudly and insistently clearing his throat. He was leaning up against the bedroom doorframe with a smirk on his face.

"I'd say, get a room you two but..." He raised both hands, palms up and shrugged, his eyes trailing around the edges of the room.

"And I'd say, do you like to watch, perv?"

Niki dropped her chin to her chest and wiped her mouth with the back of her hand, smiling.

"You ready, Jess? I want to do this before dinner."

"Sure, be right there."

I looked at Niki unpacking her suitcase. "Are you alright if I leave for an hour or two? Jimmy wants to have a chat. You and Sarah can get to know each other better."

"Sure, babe. Take your time. I know you guys have a bunch to catch up on. Oh, and by the way, you realize you're leaving me alone with an angry and highly hormonal pregnant woman. So if I'm missing when you get back, check the backyard for buried bodies. "

I gave her a sweet kiss and said, "You're the best, Niki." I took her by the hand and led her back to the family room, where I left her with Sarah who sat on the couch, mumbling expletives and something about killing Jimmy. Niki gave me the 'you owe me big time' look and I darted out of there before she changed her mind.

CHAPTER 20

Jesse

I watched Jimmy's face contort across the clear table at the local bar. Our hands were locked together in clawed fists, elbows placed level on the surface to ensure no chance of an unfair advantage, or more leverage. Jimmy had challenged me to an arm wrestling match, just like when we were teenagers. He used to be the champion of these little testosterone matches, but I'd been working out with my private trainer, Chase, back in California, getting my hand ready for racing.

"Give up, wussy?" I saw a hint of a smile. I knew he wouldn't be able to laugh and push at the same time.

He clenched his teeth and groaned one last time before he released his grip. We both laughed and it felt good to be with my big brother again, when he wasn't cussing me out for some shit I did to mess things up.

"You look good, Jesse." He reached over and snatched his beer from the edge of the table, where it had been moved out of the way for the arm wrestling. "And in better shape too." He gave a chuckle and swallowed his beer.

"California has been good for me. I guess my ole brother's advice wasn't so bad after all?"

"Well, when I open my mouth, I'm right."

I snort laughed and relaxed back in my chair. The cool brew felt good sliding down my throat.

"What's up with your girl, Niki? She's cute and very sweet. Hope you're not going to be the usual dickhead and break her heart."

"You see how I've changed on the outside. I look healthier, I'm all tan but what's changed the most is inside and it's all because of her. She does something that no one else has ever done. She makes me want to be better person. Call me crazy, but I'm fucking keeping this one."

"You're a lucky bastard all right. So have you thought about the future? You're going to be racing all over the world before long. Will she be your puppy and follow along?"

"She has plans to be a fashion designer. But I was thinking…"

"Oh shit, you - thinking? Did it hurt?"

"Asshole. Anyway, I was thinking, where is the best place for someone to study fashion?"

"You tell me, I don't make a habit of painting my toenails. What do I know about fashion stuff?"

"It's in Europe, you duffus. The exact place I will be

racing next year. So why not have her come with me? She can do her fashion thing while I race. I'll be racing in the biggest cities all over Europe."

I leaned back and took a self-righteous gulp of beer, satisfied with my plan to have Niki with me. The idea of leaving her in California while I was in Europe led to too many crazy thoughts in my pea sized-brain. Too many, 'what if's, too many temptations for her to forget about me. I would fucking fall apart without her. I studied Jimmy's face for signs of acceptance.

"Yeah, well..." Jimmy scratched his chin as he drew out the words. "You know women, just when you think you've got them all figured out... I mean, think about it, she'll be dependent on you. Is that what she wants?"

"I don't see it that way." I leaned forward, elbows on the table. "Jimmy, this is a fucking awesome opportunity for her. She'd be right in the center of a place that's important to her career dream. If I can help her with that, all the better. Shit, who knows about the future. It's not like we are getting married or anything."

Jimmy pushed his hand through his hair, letting it rest a moment at the back of his neck.

"I know, but Jess, let's just say... in the past you haven't made the brightest decisions about things. I'm just saying, bro, be cautious. Plus her family might have different plans for her."

I twirled the empty glass in my hand and a little smile crossed my face. I remembered the night I met her dad at Cinnamon's birthday party. "I'm not exactly on the A-list with her dad but…I trust her, when she says she wants to be with me."

I raised a finger and my empty glass to call for the waitress.

"Well, just keep your guard up - bob and weave - and don't get hurt, man. We've all heard about these L.A. girls…they can be tough to figure out."

"Tell me about it, bro, but Niki is different, I trust her completely."

The waitress brought us two more beers.

Jimmy's face turned serious. "It's crazy about Kenny. How do you cope with it all?"

"Honestly, I try not to think about it too much. But it's funny, now that I know he is my dad, I suddenly see so much of myself in him. It's crazy. I can't really blame him for something that happened so many years ago. It wasn't just his fault. Stuff like that just happens. You can't contain young love."

"I'm glad you're taking it so well, because I really brought you here to talk about Mom." A small shiver of alarm ran through my body. It had better not be bad news. I wanted nothing more in the world than for her to be well again.

"She's getting better. The doctor says she can go home, but she will need a little supervision at least for the first two weeks."

I relaxed, unaware that I'd had a death grip on my beer glass. "Yeah, Manny told me about it when he was in LA last week. You couldn't tell me first? Something happened to your phone?"

"Give me a break, man. It's not like my life has been a bed of roses lately. Besides, I wanted to tell you in person. She's been cooped up there for way too long. It tears me apart knowing she had to be in that place. I don't know how she can stand it."

"You and me both, brother."

"Anyway, you know the situation. If she still had her house she could have been in the day-program, come and gone each day, but with no one to drive her back and forth every day, that's the way things had to be. I talked to her last week and she's excited to get out of there and spend some time with you."

"Me? What do you mean? I'm the sorry son of a bitch who's never here." I'd caught an endless wave of grief about it from Jimmy in the past.

"Listen, here's my idea; winter is right around the corner and you know winter in New York is cold as a witch's tit, not to mention depressing. The last thing we want for Mom is for her to go through the gloomy, depressed time of year. Why doesn't she come with you, at least for a little while, until you leave for Europe or wherever you are going? "

I blinked, frozen in thought for a moment. I could feel Jimmy's pleading eyes on me. Damn, I had just lined up my training schedule.

"My racing..."

"It would only be for a month or so, until she adjusts to everything." I chewed my lower lip. I'd feel like such

210

an ass if I said no.

"Look, that place has kept her sheltered, protected her against the reality of daily life. You don't want her to have a relapse and get all depressed in an apartment by herself or something. She can't just go out and not have any support from family."

"I guess I just assumed she would stay with you and Sarah."

"I can't give Mom the attention she needs with a newborn around. I can take a little time off from work but that's going toward the baby, not Mom. I think Sarah deserves that. I'd feel like I was cheating her if I weren't focused on her and the baby one hundred percent. You know what I'm saying? Besides, we don't have the room. That one extra bedroom you guys are staying in is the baby's room."

"So what are you suggesting?"

"Why don't you take Mom to California? Kenny has an extra bedroom doesn't he? She can stay there. Three or four weeks tops. Let her get some California sun. Look at the wonders it's done for you. You are a freaking saint now."

My mind whirled with different scenarios, how this could work. I tipped my glass to drain another couple ounces of beer, as if that would help me think.

I set the glass down and said, "That's a lot of responsibility. She tried to commit suicide, what if she tries again?"

"The doctors put her on medication and there's no

way he would release her if that were the case."

I nodded and took in a deep breath. "It all sounds good, but things will be hectic when I go back, with the transplant, and Kenny is in chemo. I hope I can give her enough attention."

Jimmy reached over and placed his hand on my shoulder. The look in his eyes was soft and reassuring. "Listen bro, she just wants a little love. Trust me. She feels bad about failing you. If you can show her you don't hold it against her, that would mean so much to her."

My eyes were glued to my beer glass. My throat tightened with guilty emotions. I loved my mom. I realized that it was her depression that made her seem distant, all those years. But I had one particular childhood memory I held onto, of her gentle times. I'd play it over in my mind, every once in a while, so as not to forget. I was only a kid, not tall enough to meet her eyes. She'd lean down and kiss me on the top of my head and pull me into a hug. With her hand cupping the back of my head, I'd bury my face into her soft shirt and wallow in the bliss of motherly love. I couldn't let her down now. I swallowed more beer to wash away the lump in my throat.

"Shit. Here I was, thinking I abandoned *her*."

"You didn't abandon her. You're young, you have your career, and no one ever blamed you for anything, man. She's damn proud of you, Jesse. Her depression…it's nobody's fault. That's what her doctor explained to me. Don't play the blame game. That'll get you nowhere but knee deep in a steaming pile of shit."

I chuckled. "What the fuck, you're right, Jimmy. Mom and I could spend a little healing time together. And Kenny actually does have an extra bedroom for her." I slapped my hand, palm down on the table top. "Let's do it."

Jimmy damn near looked like he was going to cry and said, "I can't tell you how much I freaking love you, right now, for getting your act together, Jesse. Looking across this table I see my brother again. I don't know what happened, but you better stick with this girl, cause she's gold."

"She's a damn angel. I promise I'm not going to fuck things up like before."

CHAPTER 21

Jesse

My heart was racing. Sweaty palms gripped the wheel of the rental car. I watched the familiar houses and buildings pass by as Niki and I drove to the care facility to talk to Mom. I filled Niki in on the plan Jimmy proposed yesterday and she agreed. I glanced over at her as I nosed the car into a parking space. I needed her eyes right now, to steady me. I took a breath and relaxed. I sat for what seemed like an eternity, with my hands still glued to the wheel.

"I don't know if I can do this."

"You can, baby. You're stronger than you think. She needs you in her corner." Her soothing words relaxed me a little.

"You're right; you're right, absolutely right. I'm not the little kid brother anymore. I need to man up and be there for Mom."

Once inside the care facility, a friendly yet mundane looking woman showed us to my mom's room. The interior of the facility was sterile and institutional, but not as bad as I had thought. I got the creeps anyway, though, picturing my mom in here for much longer.

"Hey, Mom." She was sitting in an overstuffed brown chair, much like one you would find in a family room, reading a book. At least the chair looked cozy; it didn't matter that it clashed with the other dormitory style furniture.

"Jesse! Oh my God! I can't believe my eyes."

I was relieved to see her eyes were bright and she smiled easily. She stood up and I gave her a big hug. "Mom, this is my girlfriend, Niki. She's from L.A. …but don't hold that against her."

"Oh Jesse, funny as always. Nice to meet you, Niki." She smiled and gave me an inquisitive look.

"So nice to meet you too, Mrs. Morrison." Niki said.

"Oh, call me Emily, sweetie. Sit down. I'm sorry the only place to sit is on the bed." She took her seat in the large chair.

I cleared my throat and jumped right in. "So, Mom, I hear you get to come home."

"Yes, it looks like I'm being released to the 'normal' people." She gave a little laugh. "How about that, I'm suddenly normal." She raised her eyebrows and Niki and I smiled.

"I talked to Jimmy about it and he suggested you and I take a vacation."

"Vacation? What are you talking about?"

"You know he has the baby coming, and I would love to spend some time with you before my motorcycle training starts. And Niki needs to get back to fashion school in L.A., so I want you to come stay with me for a few weeks. A little California sunshine would do you a world of good."

"Oh Jesse, I can't do that. That's all the way across the country! I'm not the type to go off all willy nilly and travel like that. I don't want to impose on you and your girlfriend. Besides, where would I stay?"

"You'd stay with me, at Kenny's, he has an extra room."

She gasped and said, "No, I can't stay with Kenny. You don't know what you're asking."

"Why not?"

She looked down to her lap and twisted her fingers together. "It doesn't matter, but I just can't."

"Listen, Mom, Kenny's hardly going to be there. He will be in the hospital for his cancer treatment."

Her head snapped up in surprise, her eyes wide. "What? Cancer?"

"Jimmy didn't tell you?"

"No. Why didn't anyone tell me?"

Oh shit, this wasn't good. I needed to do some damage control, pronto. But maybe I could use it to my advantage.

"He has leukemia and he's very sick and he might not make it more than a month. Don't you want to go with me and see him one more time?"

Niki smiled and I felt her elbow in my side. My mom sat for a minute with an empty look in her eyes.

"Mom, are you there?"

She scratched her head and pushed her hair out of her eyes. "Oh, my. I just…this is so much to take in. Just give me a moment to think."

I stepped over in front of her chair and bent down on one knee, laying a hand on hers. I looked her in the eyes. "Mom, I would love to spend some time with you. Will you please come to California with me?"

"But what about Jimmy? I thought…"

"Mom, Sarah's about to have her baby…I want you to come."

She took a deep breath, looked up at the ceiling, and after a few more moments of silence, exhaled and said, "Alright. I'll come." She forced a smile as I stood up. "I have nowhere else to go. May as well come and be the meddlesome mother in your life in California."

"Good. We leave on Friday. Do you need us to help you pack?"

"Do I look like I'm seventy years old? I can pack my own bags."

"Okay, okay. I was just offering."

I gave her a peck on the cheek and we all said good-bye. Niki and I left her standing in the door of her room, her hand touching her mouth, looking happy, yet bewildered.

"See you Friday morning."

CHAPTER 22

Jesse

The jerk from the turbulence jolted Niki, sitting next to me. She pulled off her headphones. "Wow, you think it's going to be like this all the way to LA?"

"This is nothing. You should have seen the turbulence I once experienced on my way to Paris."

"Yeah, you keep mentioning that. What kind of turbulence was it?"

"Well, nothing like this, that's for sure," I grinned. "So are you sure I didn't scare you away yet. I mean, that was some hectic trip, with the baby and all."

"He is so adorable, but huge. I can't believe he came out of...you know...Sarah."

"I know." Jesus Christ. "I'm so glad I'm a guy. I mean, oh my God..."

"Yeah, yeah, I get the picture, Jesse. Trust me, if men were the ones to give birth, I'm pretty sure we would be extinct by now. You guys can't handle the pain."

I didn't answer. She was spot on. Men can take the pain of a punch to the face, kicks and bruises from a fight, or even a gunshot wound. But when it comes to internal organs, like a stomach ache or earache, we turn into whining little crybabies.

By the time the plane landed in LAX, I had managed to put all my doubts and worries behind me. The plan for Mom to come to Santa Monica was going like clockwork. There was a little turbulence on the plane but, overall, the flight gave Niki and me a long time to talk with my mom and for the two of them to really get to know each other.

Once we reached Kenny's house, Mom seemed a little nervous, but Kenny was already checked into his hospital room for his bone marrow transplant procedure and the house was empty. She walked in the door and looked around his living room like she was Alice and had just fallen down the rabbit hole.

My part in the procedure would only require that I go into the hospital on the day of the transplant, to make my donation. Shit, it sounded like I was going to drop off old clothes at the Goodwill. I tried to think of it that way, since the idea of a big ass needle sucking shit out of my pelvic bone kind of turned my stomach. Niki offered to drive me and hold my hand through the entire ordeal, like I was a pussy and couldn't stand the pain. I had been through worse pain riding Motocross. I just wanted to be with her. I wanted her with me all the time. Hell, I wanted her to be with me when I brushed my teeth or went for a haircut. Okay, I hardly ever get my hair cut, though I should. I just don't give a shit and Niki seems to like my hair long.

But the doctors had assured me that I wouldn't feel any pain and could leave the hospital that same day. Doctors are sneaky bastards though, they always promise no pain, then squeeze your balls or some shit like that.

I told Mom that Kenny would probably be in the hospital for weeks so she could take it easy and not worry about what to say to him after all this time. She suggested going to see him, but then changed her mind. I understood. Said she had to prepare herself first, so I let it go at that. She would tell me when she felt ready, no rush. I was just glad to have her around.

The roll-up garage door was strung with a brightly colored banner that welcomed Kenny home the day he was released from the hospital. He was pretty weak and slept a lot, but my mom was happy as a clam playing nursemaid to him in his waking moments. I wasn't sure if they'd had much time to talk.

Almost every minute of my day was spent at Rookies, where Chase and I handled all the usual daily duties of running a business. Niki was a sweetheart and even came in after her classes to pitch in for a couple hours. Though I truly appreciated her efforts, I hoped her visits were more of an excuse to see me than anything else.

She even made Kenny a gag gift that she gave him before he went for his procedure. It was a fancy designer hospital gown she made for him to wear instead of those horrible rags with two strings they give people to wear. I don't think he really wore the damn thing but I thought it was a brilliant business idea.

Everyone came to the party; Chase, Kat and a few old friends of Kenny's from here in the Santa Monica area. It wasn't the exact day he was released from the hospital, because we had to wait until he felt well enough to handle the excitement. The patio was decorated with colorful balloons and Niki had ordered a really nice cake from the bakery, decorated for the occasion. We had wanted to have the party at Rookies but Kenny hadn't felt ready for that yet.

Kat had brought her guitar and, as the sun was setting and the party died down, we sat around the family room listening to her play and sing a couple of her songs.

Niki was snuggled next to me on the couch, my arms around her, and half-finished plates of cake were left on the coffee table. Niki wiggled her shoulder against me, giving me a nudge, and glanced at my mom as she stood up to carry a dirty plate to the kitchen.

Niki whispered in my ear, "Babe, maybe you should go check on your mom. She seems a little sad."

I heard the clatter of plates in the sink and stretched

my neck up to look over the top of the couch. I saw her disappear into her bedroom but she didn't shut the door.

"Go. I'll clean up here."

I nodded and released Niki from my arms.

I poked my head into her room. "Mom, are you okay?"

"I'm fine, Jesse. Just seeing Kenny back home... you don't understand. It's just very emotional for me. Thank God you were a good donor match."

"I was a *perfect* match, and yes thank God I was. But Mom, I have to tell you something I haven't mentioned yet. When I was tested to see if I was a match, the hospital told me something I couldn't believe. They told me I was a match for my dad."

"What do you mean? How would they know? Your father is dead, my dear."

"No, you don't understand. They told me that Kenny is my dad."

Her face went white and she choked, trying to suck in air.

"Mom, why didn't you ever tell me that Kenny could be my dad?"

"Oh my dear Lord, Kenny is your dad?" She covered her face with her hands and wiped her palms down its surface, like she wanted to wipe away the years of secrets.

"You never knew?"

"I didn't... I...I may have suspected but..." She rubbed her palms on her thighs as she sat on the edge of the neatly made bed. She shook her head and looked up to the ceiling, as if praying for the courage to say what she needed to get off her chest.

"What happened, Mom? I really need to know. Why did things go the way they did? What happened between you and Frank…and Kenny?"

"Oh Jesse, dear. I didn't want to hurt you. I didn't want you to think poorly of me. I was under so much pressure from your grandmother and Frank, and well, everybody. I didn't know what to do. I was young and stupid…and stupidly got pregnant. You must think horrible things about me."

"No, Mom. Never." I pulled up the small decorative chair from the corner. "Kenny told me that part."

"He did?"

"Yeah, Kenny and I had a heart to heart when all this shit came down about his cancer."

She closed her eyes and massaged her forehead with two fingers, pinching the area right between her eyebrows. "Oh, I see." Her voice was low but she continued. "Like I said, Jesse, I was young and stupid and got pregnant out of wedlock. This was in a time, and in a small town, where that sort of thing was frowned upon." She paused. "Then there was the horrible accident…and everything changed in my life in the blink of an eye. The whole Earth just opened up beneath my feet and swallowed me into darkness."

"What happened with the accident, Mom? What really happened?" She looked like she was about to cry.

"Don't be upset, Mom. Kenny told me everything about Dad. The way he treated you was atrocious. Kenny explained it. Dad wasn't a good husband. I can understand that it must have been difficult to love him and, with the added pressure from Grandma, you felt you could never divorce him. You were stuck. You had so many reasons to give in to your feelings and emotions towards Kenny, but couldn't."

"You don't know it all. Frank may have been a bad husband but what I did was even worse."

"Mom, like I said, we're all human and you were just... following your heart."

She leaned forward and grabbed my wrist. Staring into my eyes she said, "Listen Jesse, it's not what you think. There is more. Much more. I did something horrible. Are you sure you want to hear everything?" Letting go, she leaned back and took a deep breath.

Her response shook me but there was no going back now so I nodded. I needed to hear the truth, finally.

"It all happened on the Fourth of July in 1996. We were having a great time at my friend Lisa's party and your dad was getting drunk, as usual. He wanted to leave because that's what he did when he got drunk. I told him not to drive. Then I realized he had put you and Jimmy in the car. I got you boys out...he was so drunk he couldn't even get the key in the ignition."

"What happened next?"

CHAPTER 23
Fourth of July 1996

Emily

Frank was such an asshole!

I sat with my back against Lisa's front door. I could barely breathe. The thought of Frank taking the kids while he was drunk had left me shaking and scared out of my wits. I held Jimmy and Jesse close to me, waiting for my breath to return to normal, looking up at the ceiling. *I hope no one sees.* But Lisa did.

She rushed over to help me to my feet. Lisa probably knew. No one talked about these things, no one wanted to confront the ugliness, bring it out in the open, because then you had to make a decision and take action, do something about it. It's just easier for everyone to keep quiet, ignore it, and hope it will just go away on its own. You fool yourself and you hope you can fool everyone else, but they know. The look in Lisa's eyes told me she wanted to help but chose to suffer for me, in silence, right along with the rest.

"Are you okay, Emily?"

"I'm fine. Can you watch the kids for a while? I need to go back and make sure Frank doesn't drive home drunk."

"Sure, Em. Take all the time you need." She gave me a concerned look but smiled for the sake of the boys and corralled them back to the party.

I smoothed my hair and slipped out the door to the car. Frank was just sitting there, in the driver's seat, slumped over the wheel. I couldn't tell for sure if he had passed out, so I pulled the door open and shoved at his shoulder. "Frank, move over, I'll take you home."

He wasn't completely out yet and he groggily said, "Wha-a-a...what?"

"Move over!" I shoved harder hoping to shake him awake. He started to move but fumbled and it took him two attempts to slide over the bench seat of our old beater car.

"You're a bitch. Stop shoving me."

"Yeah, yeah, just—move—over."

I managed to get behind the wheel and started the ignition. I pulled out of the driveway at Lisa's rolling estate and pointed the car in the direction of home. Frank continued to make it practically impossible to drive, yelling, cursing and nearly falling into me as I drove.

"You were flirting with that son of a bitch gigolo in there. You wanted to fuck him, didn't you? But you don't want to fuck me anymore, do you?"

"Just shut up, Frank. You're always drunk. Maybe if you weren't drunk all the time…"

"That's typical of you frigid women… blame the husband," he slurred. I looked over at his red, watery eyes as his head wobbled in drunkenness. I couldn't believe it. He had managed to bring a can of beer. He snorted a disgusting laugh and tipped the can, shaking the last drops into his mouth.

"You're calling *me* frigid, you piece of shit. You with your limp dick from drinking…" I was so sick of this. The same old game, the same old argument. My stomach twisted with anger. I knew I should keep my voice calm, but I couldn't stop the rage that was building inside. My blood was boiling and the madder I got, the more my voice began to rise. "You're an asshole, Frank. You don't take care of me…" I spat the words loudly.

"Bitch, you don't take care of me, *or* the kids… they hate you. They told me so. They said, 'Mom is always crying, blah, blah, blah…' They're right, Emily. You're always crying and whining. You need to be a wife for once, a real wife. You have duties, like when's the last time you sucked my dick, bitch?"

Hot tears were stinging my eyes. My kids didn't say that, did they? My kids loved me. Thoughts of desperation clutched at me like a hand around my throat, suffocating me. What kind of life was this? How could I have been so foolish and chosen the wrong guy?

By now, tears ran in torrents down my face, blurring my vision. I tried to wipe them away with the back of my hand but it was difficult with Frank's yelling and swaying. He flailed his arms as he ranted like a man possessed and he kept bumping into me, making it difficult to steer the car.

With all the distractions I swerved a little. But it was late on a holiday evening and the road was empty of cars. It was only a minor digression from my lane, but it inflamed Frank's rage all the more, adding fuel to the fire he was building in which to burn me in effigy.

"What the hell are you doing, bitch? You can't even drive."

As the car corrected on the road, his body leaned into mine. He grabbed my wrist. In his drunken stupor he probably imagined that he was taking control of the wheel to get the car back on the road, but in reality the car had barely swerved.

"You're going to get us fucking killed."

No sooner were his words of prophecy out of his mouth, when he pulled down hard on the steering wheel. The tires screeched. The car jerked violently to the side on the simple, small town, two-lane back road.

The old beater car - built in the years of no airbags, when lap belts were the only kind of seatbelt, for people too poor to afford any better - swerved off the road and hit a massive oak tree, head on. My lap belt was fastened. Frank's wasn't. I'd forgotten to remind him to put it on. All I suffered was a bruise from hitting the steering wheel, but his body was ejected from the car, crashing through the windshield, and he died.

CHAPTER 24

Jesse

My head was spinning. I sat woodenly in the chair, opposite my mom, in the small extra bedroom of Kenny's house, where she was perched on the edge of the bed facing the window. I gulped, forcing the dryness out of my mouth. My brain refused to register any negative perceptions. She's my mother, a saint in my eyes. Nothing would ever change that.

"So it was an accident." I tried to shrug it off.

"It doesn't end there."

No. No. No. I didn't think I wanted to know anymore. I wanted to put my fingers I my ears and go, 'la, la, la, la.' But she continued. She had to tell the whole, terrible truth and get it out of her head, for her own sanity's sake.

"I was scared that the police would think I was at fault. People at the party saw us fighting and knew it'd been going on for a long time. I was scared. I was desperate. I worried that the police would think I hit the tree on purpose to kill Frank. I was afraid they would take you and Jimmy away from me, or I'd go to jail, so…I covered it up."

"Oh my God, Mom, what did you do?"

"I made it look like he was driving. The windshield was only broken on the passenger side so I had to do something about that. I took a rock, a big rock I found on the side of the road and, from the inside, I smashed the rest of the windshield. And then I walked away.

"When I got back to Lisa's house I told her that Frank had hit me in the face and that's how I got the bruise on my head, that we had a big fight and he kicked me out of the car and insisted on driving home."

Mom sat hunched over, with her head hanging down in shame. I had never seen her look so defeated before. After a silence she spoke. Her voice wavered and cracked. "Jesse, I've never told this to anyone else before, but this guilt has ruined my life. At times I just wanted to end it all, to end the shame and guilt. It was the hardest thing to live with, but understand that I did it for you and Jimmy. I guess, in the long run, it didn't do any good keeping it all bottled up inside. Look where it left me, on medication and a burden to you and Jimmy. Please forgive me."

The shame she felt forced her to bury her face in her hands and she gave in to the sobs that shook her. I moved to the edge of the bed, put my arms around her and moved with her as she wept, rocking back and forth.

In a muffled voice, from behind her hands, the words poured out. She was relieved to finally tell the truth. "I just couldn't bear the thought of losing you boys. You were everything to me." She wiped her face with her hands, then dried them on her jeans and took a breath, quelling the tears. "I gave up everything to keep my baby when I found out I was pregnant with Jimmy. Your grandmother wanted me to give up the baby for adoption, but I couldn't. I loved him even before he was born. She had a fit about the pregnancy. Labels like, 'bastard child' were part of her world. She was a pretty strict Catholic and, in her book, you did the right thing and got married. So I did what a good Catholic girl should do and stayed with a worthless husband. I even gave up on going to college so you boys would have a traditional family life…I guess I was wrong. Look what it got me instead."

"Mom, Mom, Mom… this is not your fault. He caused this. You were the victim, you were always the victim in that marriage, not him. Mom, listen to me. I love you. You are everything. Nobody should treat you like he did. Nobody!"

We sat for a few moments, in silence, until she calmed down and offered a meek smile as I released her from my hug. I moved back to the little chair across from her.

"What about Kenny?" I asked. "Did you ever love him?"

"I always loved Kenny. He was the one I should

have been with."

"Why weren't you together?"

"It was complicated. We all started out as friends and, despite his horrible behavior, Kenny looked up to Frank. He was his big brother, after all…you know how that it is. And Frank wasn't always so bad. I guess having a baby at such a young age, all the responsibility…he just wasn't ready. So I did what I had to do and then after Frank died and Kenny came to help, I felt guilty every time Kenny tried to touch me or show any affection. It reminded me of Frank and what I had done."

"I think you're wrong about this guilt thing, Mom." I leaned forward, with my elbows on my knees and patted her small hand.

"Kenny knew Frank was an asshole. He told me. He said he went back to Thunder Ridge after the funeral because he loved you and he hoped you could get back together."

"I don't think so, Jesse. He would never forgive me for what I did."

There was a brief moment of silence.

"You didn't do anything wrong, Emily," a deep voice rumbled. I looked up and, from my vantage point, I saw Kenny standing just inside the threshold of the bedroom. Mom turned around. How long had he been standing in the doorway, listening?

"There's nothing to forgive. If only you had told me what happened, life would have been so different… for the both of us."

"Oh, dear Lord, Kenny. I didn't know you were here. I thought you were resting in your room."

Kenny took a few steps further into the room. I stood up and Mom did too, smoothing her blouse. I watched the two of them, anxious to see the look on her face to see if there was any hope in her eyes.

"I… I didn't know you were awake," she stammered.

I exchanged places with Kenny and made a quick retreat out the door. I had a feeling they needed to be alone for a while.

Kenny worked his way around the bed to Mom's side of the room where she stood in front of the window, wide eyed, with her mouth hanging open.

Beams of California sunlight fell across the walls, bathing the room in a warm yellow glow. Funny thing, I had never noticed before the bright appearance of the small cramped bedroom space. I took one last glance back and saw Kenny take Mom's hand in both of his. They stood face to face, smiling into each other's eyes. In the last moment before I ducked out the door, I heard him say, "Emily, my dear, how could I sleep through that story? I'm so happy you're here."

CHAPTER 25

Niki

I tapped my fingers on the surface of a small table at the side of the cramped recording studio Kat had rented. It was nothing like West Side Studios, but at least nobody was scamming her here. She was recording the vocals for her CD and I was watching her through a glass window. She stood in front of a large microphone, wearing large black headphones. I saw her mouth forming the words but I heard nothing, as I was sitting in an area where I wouldn't disturb the recording process.

Jesse was supposed to call, any minute, to let me know when he was on his way. He was taking me on another motorcycle ride, up into the hills of Hollywood to see the Hollywood sign, as soon as he could get off work. I wanted nothing more than to spend my time with my arms wrapped around his hard body, pressed up against his back, feeling the rush of the wind, instead of being in a dark boring studio. Jesse had me hooked. Who'd have thought I would get into motorcycles?

But Kat had made me, 'promise, promise, promise,' I would come and watch her record. After her last bad experience at this studio, she begged me to come along as her bodyguard. When we got in the car to drive over I asked her if I was supposed to be her 'muscle,' because I was certainly no threat to anyone. She told me she had her own muscles and I was her sidekick, at which I had to roll my eyes and give her a slap on the arm.

This time, thanks to Conner, the studio assistant we met the day we discovered she had been scammed, the session was going smooth. Okay, I still wanted to call him Elvis, but not in front of Kat. She seemed to like him and if I didn't get his name right, I'd catch an endless bunch of crap from her about it.

The moment the table top buzzed, from the vibration of my phone, my eyes lit up, but my mood took an immediate dive when I saw the call was from my dad instead of Jesse. I hurried out of the studio and took the call.

"Niki, I heard you were in New York."

"How did you know that?"

"I'm a lawyer, Niki. I have my ways. Why were you in New York?"

"I was with Jesse. He had a meeting with his racing team managers. Oh and Dad, I really have something I want to tell you…about being a fashion designer. I

236

know for sure…"

"Uh huh, I see…"

He was stalling. What was he doing? I had visions of him sitting at this work desk, guiding the mouse of his computer, reading emails while we were talking. It was rare for him to simply talk on the phone and not be jotting down notes or clicking on the computer screen.

"Dad, are you busy? Because if you're busy we can talk later."

"That's all good but…"

Geez, he's not even listening. Who was he talking to? I strained to hear the muffled voice of whoever he was talking to, in his office, beside me. He came back to our conversation.

"Sure, Niki let's do that. Let's have lunch and talk about a plan of action."

"Dad, I don't need your plans. I have my own."

"I know, Niki and I support them, hear me out. Come meet me for lunch. Give me half an hour of your time…I have another call…I have to take this."

"Okay, when?"

"Thursday at Spago's at 1:00."

"Alright, Dad." I scowled at my phone as I ended the call.

As I walked back into the studio a text banner popped up on the top of my phone saying Jesse was outside, waiting on the Harley. Warm thoughts replaced the sour feeling that the conversation with my Dad had left. I pounded out a reply with my finger and chucked the phone in my purse. I gave Kat the 'see ya later' wave through the recording booth window and dashed out of the recording studio, skipping down the short flight of stairs to the lobby, my excitement pushing me to forgo the elevator.

I had learned by now to wear long pants and boots for motorcycle rides and I was equipped in protective gear as Jesse drove us up the steep dirt road into the hills overlooking Hollywood. He stopped the bike at the top, as close as sightseers were allowed to get to the famous sign, and we got off to take in the view. In the past, visitors had been able to go right up to the giant letters, but unfortunately, due to vandalism and gang tagging, the sign was now enclosed in a chain link fence, with a barbed wire top.

Jesse set his helmet on the black leather seat of the Harley, next to mine. He stepped over to where I stood, admiring the stretch of green trees as a gentle wind lifted the shorter strands of my hair that had escaped from my pony tail. He slipped his arms around my waist from behind and scanned the horizon, pressing me against his body.

"Look at all those trees. Who would believe that this is L.A.?" he said in a soft voice near my ear.

I gave a nod and a barely audible, "Mmm, huh." His touch felt good, like Dreamsicles and sunshine, and I leaned into him, wanting more. He nibbled at my ear, my neck, and I turned my head as far as I could to reach for a quick taste of his lips without leaving my cocoon.

After a few minutes of silence he asked, "Babe, what's up? You're very quiet today."

I pursed my lips at the worrisome thoughts tumbling around in my head.

"My dad called, right before you came to pick me up."

He was silent and waiting. "He wants to meet for lunch and talk about my plans, which really means his plans for me."

"How bad can it be?"

"I suppose he could cut me off financially, ruin my plans for school."

"He's agreed to pay so far, but if he drops a bomb on you and says he won't pay anymore, screw him. I can pay."

"I don't think he's going to pull his support. He seems agreeable to me being enrolled at FIDM. But, even so, I don't want you to be forced to take care of me. I can take care of myself."

I envied people like Jesse, who thought life was just that easy. Although I had been striking out on my own lately, following my dreams and standing up to my dad, I had to face the fact that I was financially dependent on him. I had never had a job in my life; not even a part-time job, like working at a fast food restaurant. I needed to take my independence another step further, but how?

Kat had never had a job, other than her music gigs, either. Chase had two jobs and Jesse had his job at Rookies, though I wondered if Kenny even paid him for that since business was so slow when I first met him.

Whatever the case may be, I felt bad that I had to rely on men for my livelihood and the thought of trading one benefactor for another didn't sound like the best idea. I did not want to be indebted to him.

"I know he's up to something."

Jesse put his hand on my shoulder and turned me to face him. "Just know that I'm here for you no matter what. You can count on me."

"I know, babe."

He smiled and kissed me.

CHAPTER 26

Niki

Thursdays were my short day of classes; there was only one, late in the afternoon. I made a habit of stopping by Rookies before class, to spend some time with Jesse. Today was no different, but it was also the day I was to meet my dad for lunch.

When I arrived, Jesse was preparing the bar for the midday crowd. After a long, slow kiss of his perfectly shaped lips, I dropped my tote bag on the floor and slid onto the nearest bar stool to watch him work. He pushed his hand through his hair and I thought I might just jump right over the bar top and drag him into the back room. That move with his hand still got me all hot and bothered.

His blue eyes sparkled as he leaned his elbows onto the slick surface of the bar top and announced, "I've got some good news."

"Great, that's my favorite flavor. What is it?"

"I got a call from Laurent. The contract has now

been finalized so, guess what? You're coming to Milan with me for a whole month!" He gave me a big grin and made the 'shaka' sign. "Shaka, shaka, baby!"

My eyes grew wide as saucers. "Whaaat? That's great, Jesse, but you mean *you* are going to Milan."

"Niki, I want you to come with me, and before you say no, you can't afford it, I talked to Laurent about it and your airfare has already been calculated into the budget."

I was speechless; the idea of going to Italy with Jesse was mind blowing.

"Oh my God, Jesse, oh my God! Why didn't you say anything about this before?"

"Didn't want to get your hopes up. I wanted to run it by Laurent first and get their approval before I opened my big mouth. Just think, you could see the fashion center of Italy, hell it's probably the fashion capital of all of Europe."

"No, sweetie, Paris is, but I'll go for Milan, it comes in a close second!" I was happier than a kid in a candy store. Dare I imagine all of the possibilities of Milan? They all swam in my head, having a happy party, until logic jumped in and brought the fun thoughts to a screeching halt.

"What about my classes…school? I can't just ditch classes for a month."

Jesse came around the bar to stand next to me and cupped my face in his hands. Gazing into my eyes he lowered his voice to a sexy purr and said, "Come to

Italy with me, Niki. I want you with me. I have to be there for over a month and I don't think I can stand to be away from your sweet lips for that long."

His eyes could have been lasers, for all I knew, because they shot through me to the core and melted me into a puddle. It was difficult to form the words with my mouth, now that I was a puddle, but I stammered and said, "I...I'll have to see if I can rearrange my classes..."

I stared at my dad across the small table at Spago's restaurant, set with Italian bread and a plate of olive oil for dipping. He looked handsome in his dark suit; sharp, with the crisp white cuffs of a dress shirt peeking out of his jacket sleeves, very much the way a lawyer should look.

I narrowed my eyes. "What did you want to talk about?" I asked hesitantly. I was already convinced this scene would play out much like all the others. He talks, I listen. He checks his watch a gazillion times, then checks his phone a gazillion more. He lays down the law, which is always his way or the highway. We get interrupted and suddenly he has a pressing engagement and exits in a hurry, leaving half his food uneaten on the plate.

He started talking and cut right to the chase. He always did.

"I think I might be onto something here, Niki. You said on the phone you went to New York...how did that go?"

My stomach twisted with nervous trepidation. I imagined buckets of acid being wrung out of my internal organs. Why did it always have to be like this? I knew what he was hinting at. What he really wanted was to know about Jesse and how the two of us were getting along. It was no secret that he didn't like Jesse. Whatever his opinion was of Jesse, my choice of a guy, a job, or anything in my life, would always be the wrong one in my dad's eyes.

I closed my eyes for a moment, searching for something to give me strength. I remembered how Jesse never criticized my decisions or my career choices. I thought of how confident he was, in everything he did. Even if Jesse made a bad choice, like punching some guy in the nose, he acted with conviction and led with his heart.

I decided it was time for me to do the same. I took a deep breath and launched into my spiel, with the decision that it was better to lay it all out on the table, speak from the heart, and just be myself, because I'm a pretty damn good person, if I say so myself.

"Listen, Dad, Jesse took me to New York for business, but I had a chance to stay in the fashion design capital of the U.S. I have to tell you, it was awesome. The stores, the shops...Manhattan was fantastic. I even went shopping for fabric for my next school project. But Dad, the most amazing thing happened while I was shopping. It was kind of mystical and eerie...I got goose bumps when it happened, but don't freak out, I'm not going all hippie weird on you or anything. It's just that when I was walking through the Garment District, I had this epiphany. It was like Mom was there, when I was sorting through the fabrics imagining what I could make with them, it's like she was communicating with me. She was guiding my hands, helping me pick the right fabric, like what would go with this one, or imagine what I could make with that one.

"Dad, I know you don't really see the value in my fashion design career, but I know Mom supports me from...wherever she is. I don't mean to sound disrespectful, Dad, but whatever you have to say...I'm not going back to law school, I can't do it." I paused for a moment and stared at him again, waiting for all hell to break lose. I winced. "Are you mad at me?"

He had been chewing his food and, to my surprise, he was listening. He set down his fork, took a sip of his iced tea and cleared his throat. "As a matter of fact, Niki, that's what I was going to talk to you about. First of all, no, I'm not mad. People don't get mad, only rabid dogs go mad. People get angry. Therefore, am I angry with you? No. I understand your argument. Secondly, I have come to terms with your notion of being a fashion designer and not a lawyer. Go ahead, take your classes, sew some clothes, do whatever it is you need to do to be happy, you have my blessing."

I let out a breath. I couldn't believe it. My lawyer dad finally agreed with me on something. Maybe I should be an attorney after all. No, no. Just kidding.

"That's great, Dad. I'm glad you see it my way, because I was just given a fantastic opportunity to study abroad."

"Why that sounds wonderful, Niki. Will you be studying fashion at The University of Paris, or another university? Which one is your study abroad program coordinated with?"

"Oh, it's not through a school program, Jesse is taking me. He's going to be located in Italy for Motocross training and he's taking me along. I'm going to study fashion in Milan and all the design hot spots while he races."

"No Niki, you're not."

Well, there it was. The other shoe finally dropped. I kicked myself for thinking that anything would be different, that I could have outwitted my dad, that my happiness mattered to him for one iota.

"I would not advise such a foolish plan. You may think you know this man, but you don't. I've met the likes of him before. You would be traveling with him as nothing more than... an escort, a kept woman for his pleasure, if you know what I mean. See the writing on the wall, Niki. Instead of putting your nose in pretty boy's lap you should be putting your nose in a book and finishing this school. This Jesse guy is not virtuous,

Niki. He's the kind of guy who meets a sweet girl like you when he's too young and he fucks up because there's too much left to do. He will be sleeping around behind your back with every starry-eyed girl he meets on the road. You're better off without him. He will just mess it up for you, Niki. Trust me, I know his type. I meet guys like him every day, through my job; rock stars, musicians, actors… And I know you…"

"You don't know me and you certainly don't know Jesse. You haven't taken the time to talk to him or anything. All you did was scream and yell like a mad man and humiliate me in front of him at your house. He's a goddamn hero, he saved his uncle's life and I want to be with him."

"I'm your father and I know more about life than you do. Trust me, Jesse is just trouble on a motorcycle…You think you have a relationship with him? Ha. He's years away from having any kind of a meaningful relationship with a woman. The best thing you could do is just walk away from Jesse."

"Who are you right now? I thought you would be happy for me. You don't care about anyone but yourself. I don't care what you say, I'm still doing it."

"Over my dead body."

"You can't tell me what to do."

"Yes, Niki, I can."

"Why? Because you hold the purse strings?"

"Because I'm your fucking father, that's why."

"Ha! Some father you are."

"Jesus Christ, Niki, have some respect. I've given you everything. I put you through college, tried to pave the way for you to have a good life. I have even agreed to support you in your new career choice. I get it now; you don't want to be a lawyer, you have your own dream. I get it. And I will continue to pay your rent and cover all of your expenses. Listen, Niki, put some goddamn sense in your mind. Think about what Mom would want for you. She would want you to be smart about this and that's what I'm offering you, the smart decision."

I sat like a stone, my face expressionless, staring at the water glass in front of me as it weeped condensation, sinking into my chair like a ton of bricks had been placed on my heart.

"Here's what I'll do for you. I'll pay your rent, pay your car, phone; I'll even pay for your fashion classes. I'll let you follow your dream. When you told me about what happened in New York with your mom, I felt it too. That's why I'm going to offer you something equally as exciting. I am willing to pay for you to study in New York after you finish your FIDM classes here."

"Why would you do that, Dad?" I asked flatly. I moved like a robot just going through the motions now.

"Because you're my daughter, you're my blood. There's just one thing…" He leaned one elbow on the table, clenched his teeth and jabbed his finger at me. …you stay away from that fucker Jesse." He spat the words in a low voice, so as not to create a scene in the restaurant. "He's no good for you, Niki. Do it my way, I pay for everything. Do it your way, with Jesse...you're on your own. Give me back the car, give me back the cell phone, no more paid tuition. You'll be dropped from your classes and kicked out of that school. You think you can get a job and make it on your own, without me? You've never had a job, you have no skills to put on a resume. Who the hell's going to hire you? And that ridiculous flower child friend of yours... she won't pay your half of the rent for you.

"Think about it, Niki. Kick that fucker to the curb, he's not worth losing everything that I can give you."

He sat back into the polished mahogany chair, arrogantly cocking one arm over the backrest. He tossed his white linen napkin onto his plate and said, "What's your decision, Niki? Do you want a chance to fulfill your vision, your dreams, or would you rather be a groupie and follow him around? It's as simple as that."

CHAPTER 27

Jesse

The white teddy bear had Niki's smell all over it, elegant and sophisticated, just like her. The bear was pretty worn-out. She said it had been with her ever since she was a kid, back at boarding school. She left it at my place, the last time she slept over. The last time we lay, together, in each other's arms, skin to skin, heart to heart. I placed the bear carefully on top of the pile of clothes already packed in my suitcase and exhaled.

"You sure you've got everything, Jess?" Kenny asked.

I look down at my two suitcases. One was zipped and leaning against the bedroom door, the other was still open, on the bed, waiting for the last item to be added. "Yep, all packed. Let's roll. I'd like to get there early. I need to get my ticket first."

"I didn't take you for a teddy bear guy. Afraid of

getting homesick?" Kenny chuckled.

I lifted the furry bear from his perch on my suitcase and looked at the lopsided red bow of the ribbon around its neck. "It's Niki's. I thought it might help...you know, when I miss her." I frowned at the stupid thing, suddenly feeling foolish for wanting to take it along. "Ah, maybe not." I tossed the bear onto the bed and zipped the suitcase shut. "Be sure to give it to her when you see her, okay?"

"No problem, Jess. Hey, I'm sorry she couldn't make it, but it's a long time for her to be out of school."

"Yeah, well. There is a little more to it than just the school," I said and yanked the last suitcase off the bed.

"What do you mean? I thought you said she had to stay home because she couldn't miss a whole month of classes?"

"That's what she told me, but I had a feeling there was more to it than just that, so...I called Kat and she confirmed it. Actually, I tricked her into telling me that it's her dad who is behind it. Kat thought I already knew."

"Her dad? Oh, I see."

"Yeah, her dad still has her completely under his thumb and I guess Niki was too embarrassed to tell me. She has been trying so hard to break free from him, but he does provide a lot of things for her. Things that are tough to say goodbye to. Apparently he offered to pay for her to study fashion in New York after she finishes school here. Only the offer comes with one condition;

she can't see me anymore."

"Wow, I'm so sorry, Jess. But don't give up hope. Love is a peculiar thing and it often conquers the biggest obstacles. A lot can happen in a month. For all you know, she could be right here waiting for you when you come back."

Kenny gave me an understanding pat on my back and grabbed one of the bags. "Wow, this is heavy. What the heck did you pack in here? A body?"

"I'll get it, man. You are still weak from all the chemo, I'm sure."

I grabbed the two suitcases and heaved them into the trunk of Kenny's sporty black muscle car.

~*~*~*~

"Thanks for taking me to the airport," I said as the Camaro crept along in rush hour traffic on the 405 Freeway towards LAX.

"No worries. It's a bitch to pay for long-term parking…costs a fortune. Besides, I owe you a million more favors than a lift to the airport, for saving my life and my business."

"You sure you're ready to be back full-time at Rookies?"

"You bet I am. I can't wait. The whole reason I opened the place was because I love operating a bar, watching people be happy and have a little fun in life, even if the fun is found in that one beer at the end of the work week. I missed it and you know, Jesse, I realized while I was sick that in order for a man to be happy, he needs a purpose in his life. Something to look forward to every day or... someone." He glanced over at me with a look that made me wonder if he was talking about himself anymore.

"That's good. I'm glad Chase and I didn't fuck it all up while you were sick. So, what's going on with you and Mom? Have you two decided on how to move forward?"

Kenny looked at me. "Not really. We're just taking it slow. See what happens, you know? The flame that burned so hot many years ago might still have a little life left. We'll see." He chuckled and smiled as he spoke. I could tell he was hopeful about the possibility. I was glad that at least someone was making headway in their relationship.

"Be sure to say goodbye to Mom, will you?"

"Of course. I'm surprised she didn't come with us to see you off."

"Nah, you know mom. She isn't much for goodbyes. I guess she had her fair share."

Kenny nodded in understanding and soon after, he nosed the Camaro curbside and stopped in front of the entrance to the international terminal at LAX. "All right. Stay safe, Jess. Don't get in any trouble over there. I hear that the Italian police can be pretty tough on troublemakers."

"Don't worry. I'm a changed man now, Kenny." I

gave him a crooked smile, thinking I could have just as easily called him Dad. It was beginning to feel like his role in my life had changed, too. I took the suitcases out of the trunk, hurled them onto a trolley, and slung the backpack that would be my carry-on over one shoulder.

"Call us when you get there, so we know you've arrived safely."

"I will." We did the big bear hug goodbye and I entered the terminal, where I found a huge open area, full of milling travelers, their kids and their bags. I scouted out Alitalia Airlines and easily found the service desk where I would pick up my ticket.

The line to the ticket counter was pretty short and a couple of minutes later I gave my passport to a sharply dressed woman behind the counter.

"I'm here to pick up my ticket to Milan. My name is Jesse Morrison."

She looked up and smiled, "Let's see...Jesse Morrison. Yes, two tickets to Milan. I just need the other passenger's passport also, please."

"There's no other passenger, there was a change of plans. It will only be me flying today." I sighed and handed her my passport. Her eyes briefly flicked down to the passport, then up again to mine. I thought for a fraction of a second I saw the slightest twitch at the corner of her mouth. Was it a smile? Was she flirting?

"Thank you Mr. Morrison. Umm...I think this young lady behind you is trying to get your attention."

She nodded her head and I turned. There was Niki,

standing right behind me, her beautiful face beaming a wide smile.

"Niki! What are you doing here? I thought you had class today? Did you come to say goodbye?"

"That's a lot of questions." She laughed. "As it turns out, I won't be having classes for a while." Her eyes sparkled as she looked straight at me in anticipation.

"I hope you're not joking, because that would just be cruel." I turned completely to face her, and she looked up into my eyes.

"I'm not. I want to come with you."

"But…what about your dad and the whole, 'I'll pay for everything but only if you break up with that dude…'?"

"Kat told me you had tricked her into telling you about it. I'm so sorry I didn't tell you straight away, but I needed a little time to think about it.

"Jesse, there are only two things that are important to me and my dad is not one of them. It's you and my passion for fashion design. I had to decide which is the most important and I chose you. Besides, just because I take a break from school doesn't mean I'm giving up learning about fashion design. You showed me the importance of the 'School of Life'. When I was with you in New York, I had a taste of that. I've been in school practically my whole life. Maybe it's time to be fearless. Time to learn a thing or two from real life experiences. And I can't imagine a better place than Milan to start." She looked so sincere and more determined than I had ever seen her.

"You really mean it?"

"I mean it, baby. I love you and the thought of being away from you for a whole month, would literally kill me."

"Wait, what? Did you just say that you love me?"

"It would appear so," she answered and smiled.

I dropped my carry-on and cupped her face in my hands, pushing them into her long soft hair. "Niki, you have no idea how much I've wanted to hear those words. I love you, too. I love you, babe. I fucking love you!"

I hadn't realized that I said that last sentence so loudly. All the passengers in the near vicinity stopped and looked at us, with snickering smiles. I didn't care. I wanted to shout it from a damn mountain top.

I pulled Niki close. Her lips met mine and her kiss sang through my veins, a testament to the passion I felt within. It was magic and fireworks all rolled together in one big explosion and suddenly, all those stupid poems made perfect sense. This was what true love was all about.

My internal flight of fantasy was interrupted by Niki's sweet voice.

"Jesse, baby?"

I opened my eyes and she pulled away, settling back down on her heels.

I blinked and swiveled my head to the left and the right. Everyone around us was clapping and cheering.

In triumph, I threw my right fist in the air with a fist pump and jumped around in a circle, and shouted, "Yeah! She loves me! She fucking loves me!"

Niki dipped her head and blushed with a happy smile, touching her fingertips to her mouth. She tugged on my arm. "Come on, Romeo, let's get my ticket."

Niki was all smiles and I laughed as we stepped up to the counter again. The ticket agent pleasantly scanned Niki's passport. I nodded a 'thank you' to her and a long lock of my hair fell in my eyes. I raked my hand through my hair to push back the crazy thing and the agent gave me a big smile as she handed us the tickets.

An hour later we were sitting in first class on our way to Italy.

I turned to Niki and asked, "Ready for our best adventure yet?"

Niki's eyes fired at me with excitement. "I was born ready, babe. Carpe Diem. Let's seize the day."

THE END

If you want more Jesse, you should check out my other series, Deceived. In Deceived Part 2 – Paris, we meet Jesse in a very sexy scene, a year earlier on a flight to France, to compete in Supercross De Paris.

Please help spread the word about Jesse and Niki. Tweet about it; message your Facebook friends and tell anyone else who might also enjoy it. Most importantly of all, if you could, I would love a personal review on Amazon or Goodreads by you. It really helps.

I'm so excited to hear what you think about the book, so please reach out to me on Twitter http://twitter.com/evecarterbooks or on Facebook http://facebook.com/evecarterauthor

You can also get in touch with my by email: evecarterbooks@gmail.com

Eve xoxo

Acknowledgement

First, I would like to thank all of my readers. Without you, my books would not exist. I truly appreciate each and every one of you. I would also like to give a big "shout out" to the girls in the Smutty Book Whore Mafia on Facebook. You girls rock! Without your connections and support, Deceived wouldn't have had such a good beginning. I enjoy the humor and candor with which we interact, not to mention the awesome photos. :) They give me lots of inspiration for writing my steamy sex scenes. I especially want to thank Sarah Horwath and Andrea Gregory for beta reading Fearless. Your edits and comments have been incredibly helpful.

A big "thanks" goes out to all my Twitter followers and Facebook friends, all several thousands of you, who keep me tweeting into the wee hours of the night.

Finally, I would like to thank my editor, Andrea Harding http://www.expresseditingsolutions.co.uk/ and my book cover designer, Primrose Book Design. Thanks for all of your help and clever ideas.

About The Author

Eve Carter is a true romantic at heart and with a modern contemporary erotic twist to her romance novels, you had better fasten your seatbelt, as the ride is always fun, exciting and fiery.

Living in Southern California, but a mid-westerner at origin, Eve finds plenty of inspiration for her books in her own exciting life. Eve has always loved the arts and as a young girl, she took dance classes and spent the summers reading books from the local library.

Fascinated with the written word and its power to guide the imagination, Eve started writing short stories and later took Creative Writing classes in college. Eve graduated from The University of Iowa with a B.A. in Journalism and an M.A. in Higher Education.

Made in the USA
Lexington, KY
10 June 2015